Gift

Gift

Gemma Birss

OUR STREET BOOKS

Winchester, UK
Washington, USA

First published by Our Street Books, 2012
Our Street Books is an imprint of John Hunt Publishing Ltd., Laurel House, Station Approach,
Alresford, Hants, SO24 9JH, UK
office1@o-books.net
www.o-books.com

For distributor details and how to order please visit the 'Ordering' section on our website.

Text copyright: Gemma Birss 2011

ISBN: 978 1 78099 265 5

A CIP catalogue record for this book is available from the British Library.

Design: Stuart Davies

Illustrations and cover image: Gemma Birss

Printed and bound by CPI Group (UK) Ltd, Croydon, CR0 4YY

We operate a distinctive and ethical publishing philosophy in all
areas of our business, from our global network of authors to
production and worldwide distribution.

CONTENTS

Acknowledgements

Thank you Mim and Pip for everything (especially for raising me in Zimbabwe), Katie and Niall Geoghegan for their support, Michael Mafeki Pearce for his critical eye, James Robertson for keeping it real, Jo for being the best sister, Alexandra Wenman for her constant encouragement, Edward Stopler and Bruce Stevens for celebrating with me, Nishad Kala for being my favourite and, most importantly, the Universe for bringing this all into being.

They say the skies are biggest in Africa. I can't imagine what a small sky is like; the sky is the sky. How can it be smaller than it is? When I look up at the African sky and see how endless it is, it reminds me that there are millions of different things happening to millions of different people everywhere, in every moment. It reminds me that I am only the tiniest star in this universe.

Who Am I?

Most children know where they come from. They have grand-parents, a mother and father, and ten or so brothers and sisters. They grew up together in the villages, chasing lizards, swimming in rivers, exploring the bush and going to school to learn about the Chimurenga, the great war of Zimbabwe. They eat sadza every evening with their families around the fire, and then they go to sleep under the billions of stars sprinkled like grains of salt across the night. There is no questioning. That's just the way it is.

But with me it was different.

One day I woke up from a nap. The sun was shining as it always does and I opened my eyes slowly to let the light in little by little. The African heat pressed down on my skin. I could hear chickens scratching and chuckling nearby. I yawned and stretched.

And then I saw Amai, who I had never seen before in my life. I stared at her, shocked, and everything fell out of my head like water spilling out of a rusted can. I rubbed my eyes and looked around me. There was dust everywhere. Dust and trees that I didn't recognize, huts that I had never seen before, and this strange, large woman whose surprise made her mouth as round as her eyes.

We were both sitting on a reed mat under a leafy msasa tree. The sun was peeping through the gaps in the leaves, watching us closely. The woman's eyes stared out at me like a pair of shiny, black beans. She rubbed her hands over her face, as if she was as shocked as I was.

'Who are you?' she asked, her mouth barely moving from a surprised o.

'I am…' Before the words trickled from my head to my mouth, I realized that I didn't know who I was. I didn't know my name, I didn't know how old I was, I didn't know where I was. The only thing I knew was that I couldn't remember anything. It was as if the inside of my head had been scrubbed clean.

'I don't know,' I wanted to say. 'I can't remember.'

And then I realized that, not only did I not know who or where I was, but also that I could not speak. My tongue was a heavy stone in my mouth and my voice was trapped like an ant beneath it. With all my strength, I tried to say something.

'Nnnnnggghhh.' That was all I could manage and it left me exhausted.

'Maiwe!' the woman peered at me closely with her bulging eyes. 'You can't speak!'

'Nnnnnnnngghhggggghghhhhhh!' I tried again, my voice straining against my tongue. No words came.

I put my hand to my mouth to check that it was still there. I could feel my lips, and I opened them to see if I still had a tongue. Carefully I touched it with my finger. It was still there. I still had a mouth and a tongue, but I could not make words.

'Poor mwana! Poor child! But where is your mother?'

I stared at her blankly. I didn't know. I couldn't remember where my mother was, or even if I had one. It was as if a desert had been blown into the cavern inside my skull.

And then, although I tried to hold them back, hot tears spilt down my cheeks and I started to sob. It was a strange, hollow sound echoing from my belly. I jumped up and ran away from her to hide on the other side of the msasa tree. Curling up like a pangolin, I squeezed my eyes shut and pressed my head between my knees.

She walked around to where I was hiding. The soles of her feet pressed down into the dust next to me. I peeped up at her.

3

She was like a giant baobab tree, with big, round eyes and a wide mouth on the top of it. I squeezed myself into a tighter ball.

'There, there, mwana. There, there, child. You are so frightened! I think you are as confused as I am. I have certainly never seen you before. I know all the children in the village but you, mwana, are a strange one. Come now. Come and hold my hand and sit with me.' She held out her big hand. I unfurled myself and took it tearfully. She led me back around the msasa tree to sit beside her on the reed mat where I had woken up moments before.

'There is no need to cry, mwana. I am your friend. My name is Amai. You are safe with me.'

Her plump voice comforted me and the tears stopped spilling. I wiped them from my cheeks.

'What we will do is this: we will wait for Baba to come home. He will be here soon, once dinner is ready. He will know what to do.' Amai squeezed my hand and pulled me closer to her. She smelt comforting, of wood fires and freshly ground mealie meal.

As I sat on Amai's lap, she tugged at my skirt.

'But I wonder, what are these strange clothes you are wearing? You are practically naked! And this little skirt — what is it made from ... rabbit skin?'

I didn't think there was anything wrong with my skirt, but I watched quietly as she tugged the blue, cotton scarf from her head and wrapped it around me. She tied it tightly under my arms so it fell around me like a short sarong.

'That will have to do for now. I don't have any children, so I have no small dresses to give you. But this scarf is better than nothing, isn't it? When we find who you belong to, I will ask them where your clothes are.' Amai tutted crossly. 'To let a child your age go with hardly any clothes... How old are you? You must be about ten! Yoh!'

The scarf felt strange against my skin. I was used to feeling the air and heat against my body and the cloth made me feel closed

in and trapped, like a moth in a cocoon. I tugged at it to loosen it a little, and Amai looked at me with a strange expression on her face.

'Where have you come from, mwana?' she asked under her breath, shaking her head.

The Snake Dream

'Come, it is nearly dinnertime and I have not prepared anything.' Amai heaved herself up from the ground and held out her hand to pull me up with her. She lead me past a troupe of scrawny chickens, past the wood fire which was burning slowly in the centre of the compound and through the small, arched entrance of the kitchen hut. It was dark inside. The air was cool and smelt of sweet straw from the thatched roof. There were wooden crates placed side by side forming a rickety shelf against the wall of the hut. On this shelf were some tin plates and cups, three cooking pots, a collection of wooden stirring sticks, and a large tin box of cooking oil. There were two baskets hanging from the thatch. One held some bright tomatoes and spinach, and the other held a powdery sack of mealie meal.

'Sadza and tomato relish. That is what we are making for dinner tonight, mwana. I hope you like it.' The thought of food made my stomach rumble. I didn't know when I had last eaten. Amai measured cups of corn meal and water into the pot for the sadza. Leading me outside to sit by the fire, she showed me how to stir the corn meal until it boiled and thickened into a strong, white paste, which gasped and plopped with hot billows of steam. As Amai chopped the tomatoes and cooked them in a black pot on the other side of the fire, I looked around me.

The compound was surrounded by pampas grass that had been dyed silvery gold by the sun. Near the msasa tree were two small huts: Amai's and Baba's. There was an even smaller hut to the left of these. This was the corn meal store. It was raised off the ground on thin, wooden stilts to keep the grain safe from hungry rats and hyenas. The latrine toilet was further off, hidden by the tall pampas grass.

Soon the air was ripe with the rich, juicy smells of cooking. Amai went into the kitchen to fetch the plates. As she clanged the tin crockery together and busied herself in the kitchen, I stared up at the sinking sky. Stars were appearing like seeds scattered in the soil. The sky saw everything that happened on the earth. The sky would know who I was, where I had come from and how I had arrived here with nothing in my head, unable to talk. If I looked up into the twilight for long enough, perhaps it would tell me.

As I stared up into the deepening blue, a swirling sensation stirred in my stomach. It felt familiar, but I didn't know what it was or where it was coming from. It grew bigger and wider, filling my whole body. It swirled up across my chest, into my throat and finally into my head. And then suddenly my ears were filled with a loud, echoing sound, like wind. It was as if I was flying through the twilight. It felt as if I had become part of the sky, and it was the first familiar feeling I had felt since I had woken up.

I was so absorbed in this feeling, in the soaring sound of it, that I didn't hear Baba arrive.

'Ah! Here you are!' Amai clapped her hands in greeting. The sensation vanished from my body, the sound of rushing air disappeared and I turned to see an old man standing by the fire beside me.

Baba had an old, lined face with sparkly eyes that were folded under deep creases. His hair was sprinkled with grey. He stared at me long and hard, scratching his head.

Eventually he turned to Amai and said, 'Who is this?'

'I found her,' Amai said simply.

'Don't talk nonsense, Amai. You don't just find children. Where did you take her from?'

'Iwe! I didn't take her, Baba. I don't know how she came here. She can't tell me. This one doesn't talk.'

Baba looked at me carefully, his lips pursed with concentration. My heart skipped a beat. Did he recognize me? Did he know where I had come from?

'Amai, I have never seen this mwana around here.'

My heart sank.

'I know that, Baba! I have never seen her either. But let us not sit about discussing this while the food is waiting to be eaten. Let's talk when our plates are full.'

Amai handed me a plate of steaming sadza and relish. For a moment, I wondered if I had forgotten how to eat. I looked slyly

at Baba who rolled his sadza into neat portions with nimble fingers and dipped them into the relish before pushing them into his mouth. Yes, I remembered how to eat. Instinct guided my hand to roll a chunk of sadza between my fingers, moisten it with the tomato stew and push the food hungrily into my mouth.

It tasted good. My hunger told me that it must have been a long time since my last meal. I closed my eyes and concentrated on the taste of sadza and relish, to see if I recognized it. Surely if I remembered how to eat, the taste of food would also be familiar. Perhaps it would jolt a memory of my mother, who must have cooked for me as Amai had cooked this meal. My mind was blank. If I had ever eaten sadza and tomato relish before, the memory of it remained locked away.

'Let me tell you how I found her, Baba,' Amai spoke. I opened my eyes, eager to hear Amai's story, and pushed some more sadza into my hungry mouth.

'I was grinding the corn as usual and, listening to the Christmas beetles buzzing, I began to feel dozy in the heat. I left the grinder and took my mat to sit in the shade of the msasa tree. I closed my eyes, just for a short while.'

Amai yawned and closed her eyes to demonstrate, in case we hadn't understood her so far.

Baba coughed impatiently. 'Amai, is your afternoon nap important? Or can you just get to the point?'

He winked at me and I stared hard at Amai, urging her to continue.

Amai opened her eyes, took another mouthful of sadza and chewed slowly, her eyebrow arched indignantly at Baba. I was about to crack with anticipation.

'Well...?' urged Baba.

'My story is important, Baba. The more you interrupt me, the longer I will take to tell it. Now, where was I? Ah yes... Before I knew it, I was, asleep and dreaming. Eeeeh! It was a strange dream, Baba. There was a green snake. It was a bright green, like a mamba, and it had black, shining eyes like marbles in its head. It wrapped itself around my leg and it said, "Here is a gift for you, Amai." Well, that is what it sounded like. It had a whispery voice, you know how snakes hiss? But before I could ask the snake to repeat itself, do you know what it did? It bit me on my leg! Yoh! I woke up with a shout!'

Amai kicked her plump leg up in a re-enactment of her dream and I jumped, nearly spilling my meal.

'And then I saw her, this little one, curled up beside me, fast asleep. I wondered for a moment if the snake had really given me a gift from my dream. But no, that could not be possible. This little girl was not a dream. She is real. As you can see.'

'Amai, this story about your dream is very interesting, but you still haven't told me where she has come from!'

'But that is all I know, Baba. That is the end of the story. I looked around me for a clue, but there was nothing. Everything was as it had been before I had fallen asleep. There was no one around. The sun had not moved much in the sky. There was just me and this little girl.'

Baba gazed into the fire, deep in thought. It was strange to hear Amai telling this story about me. I wracked my brain for some memory that would echo Amai's sequence of events, something that might give me a clue as to how I had arrived.

Baba mopped up the last of his relish with a chunk of sadza.

'Well, there must be a logical explanation. As much as you would love to think so, Amai, I do not believe that a snake from your dream gave you a daughter. This is what we will do. We will take this little one around the village after dinner. We will ask every family if they know her, or if they know anyone who is missing their daughter. Someone must have heard something. You don't just lose a child and not say anything about it. We must find her relatives. There is someone out there who has lost their little girl and we must return her to them.'

'Yes, Baba. That is a good idea. Although when we find them, I will have a strong word with them. This little girl came to me looking like a wild animal, with uncombed hair and a rabbit-skin skirt! If she was my daughter…'

'I know, Amai, but she is not. She is someone else's daughter, and we must take her home.'

They both turned to look at me as I chewed the last of my sadza with bulging cheeks.

The Ancestor

By the time we had cleaned the pots and plates with water that Amai had fetched from the river, night was curling up around us. We left our compound to visit the neighbours.

The sounds of a family chattering around the fire reached us as Amai, Baba and I made our way along the moonlit path. I strained to hear familiarity in the voices, but my efforts were interrupted by a glimpse of something that was moving on the edge of the path, just in front of me. A narrow head emerged, followed by a long, slow, slinky body. I froze as a snake glided into the centre of the path. A choked shout broke through the evening calm. It was the haggard sound of fear rising in my own throat.

Amai whirled around to see where the shout had come from, and Baba stumbled into the back of me. Their eyes followed my pointed finger towards the green snake, shining like water in the moonlight. No one moved as it turned its black, glittering eyes on me. I held my breath, waiting for it to raise its head and strike me.

An eternity seemed to pass while the snake held me in its unblinking stare. Goosebumps prickled against my skin. No one moved. The snake slowly glided towards me, nudging its way through the dust. I was so terrified that I couldn't breathe, let alone move. My eyes were fixed on the snake's glittering, green head.

'Still, mwana. Stay still,'

muttered Baba in a sand-soft voice.

The snake drew closer and closer until its head was a millimetre from my foot. Its nose nudged against my toe. I felt its forked tongue whisper on my skin and an electric jolt of terror flew up my leg. It took all of my concentration to remain still. My heart was like a trapped butterfly beating its wings against my ribs, and the thought that the snake would hear its thuds and bite me fluttered anxiously around my head. The snake turned its head up to stare at me. I waited. Baba and Amai waited.

And then, as smoothly as it had crossed my path, it turned away and slid shyly back into the pampas grass.

Once it had disappeared, air rushed back into my lungs and Amai's voice, high-pitched with terror, crashed through the tension.

'Yooh! Baba! Mwana! Watch out there! It's the snake from my dream!' Jumping up and down, Amai picked up a stone from the path and threw it into the grass after the snake to scare it off. Baba snatched me up onto his back away from the danger. Amai turned to us, her eyes wide. 'That is the one. That is the snake that bit me in my dream. It has come out of my dream and now see, it is there, to bite us in real life!'

As I watched the snake disappear deep into the Zimbabwean bush, I wondered what it meant. The memory of the snake's flickering tongue still throbbed in my toe. Was it really the same snake from Amai's dream and, if it was, did it know where I had come from?

'Ah! Amai! Baba! It's you! What is going on here? We heard someone shouting!'

I looked down from Baba's back at the group of three strangers that had gathered around us. They must have come from the compound nearby, the people whose voices we had heard moments ago. They clapped their greetings to Amai and Baba. There was an older man, his face mapped with wisdom, and a younger couple. The woman had a sleeping baby strapped snugly to her back. The moon was bright enough to study their faces clearly, and my heart sank. I had never seen them before.

Once Amai had told them about the snake, we stood in silence for a while.

Then the old sekuru spoke up. 'That one is an ancestor,' he said in a chicken-scratched voice. We turned to look at him. 'The snake, it is a spirit messenger. Snakes don't come out at night. We all know this. The moon is too cold for them. But that one has a message from the ancestors. That is why it is here. There is no need to be frightened. It is not here to harm us. Only to deliver the message.'

Once again, silence poured into the gaps between us. I felt the cold flicker of the snake's tongue against my toe again and shuddered.

'That might be so, sekuru. But the snake has gone now, and that is not the reason Amai and Baba came to visit us this evening. And I see they have brought a young visitor with them. So let us stop chatting here about the snake and let us move back to the fire.'

The woman nodded for us to follow her as she led the way back towards the compound. Baba set me gently back on the path, but kept a firm grip on my hand as we followed her. I glanced back at the moonlit path to see if the snake was following us. Apart from our dusty footprints, the path was empty.

The fire was glowing cosily when we arrived. I stood close to Amai, my heart knocking against my chest like an eager visitor on a door. The sleepy faces of children were lit up by the soft glow of the fire. I didn't recognise any of them. The family ushered us nearer to the warmth. The grown-ups had a short discussion in low voices. Then they all turned to stare at me. Their faces were blank. Not a flicker of recognition sparked in their eyes. They didn't know me.

My heart sighed.

Amai and Baba bid their farewells and we left for the next compound.

We visited all the compounds in the village and it was always the same. No one knew me, but everyone speculated.

'Maybe she walked over from Chivhu?'

'She's too young and that is too far. Look at her skinny, little legs!'

'Her mother might have abandoned her,'

'But she is such a sweet, little thing. Who would abandon her?'

As the conversations went around and around in spirals, my thoughts returned to the snake. What message did it have to give me?

The last compound we visited was that of Tete Precious's family. It was late by the time we reached them. The fire had settled and had become a pile of glowing embers. The family was sitting around it with satisfied faces. The children were all getting up to go to bed. I watched the oldest girl lead a smaller one, who was struggling with a heavy limp, towards their hut. The two disappeared inside and then the older one reappeared alone, having put her sister to bed.

She looked up. Our eyes met and she stopped dead, her body as tense as a startled hare. She stared at me with huge eyes. She looked slowly over towards the grownups and then back at me. My heart toitoied in my chest. Did she recognize me? I started to walk across to her, but she turned quickly and retreated into her hut.

Tete Precious called out, 'Tendai, are you there?'

A small voice wheedled out, 'Yes, I am

here. I am getting ready for bed.'

'Come out here and talk to us, please, Tendai. We need to ask you something.'

The girl reappeared and shuffled towards Tete Precious, Babamukuru, Amai and Baba. She didn't even look in my direction.

'Tendai, Amai found this little girl today. She has lost her voice and we must return her to her family. Do you recognize her? Have you seen her at school?'

Tendai looked at me with a calculated blankness and shook her head fiercely. 'No. I have never seen this girl before.'

'Are you sure, Tendai?'

'Yes, I am sure, Amai,' she said. She gave me a sideways glance. I stared back at her. She *did* recognise me. I was sure of it.

'Thank you, Tendai. Good night, now. Off to bed.'

Tendai quickly turned and ran back to her hut to join her sisters. I wanted to run after her, but it was pointless. I couldn't speak. I would have to wait for another opportunity. I stayed with Amai.

'We have been everywhere in the village, Tete Precious. Nothing. No one has seen this little one before. What are we to do?'

'Maybe her family is in Chivhu, although I don't know how she came here from there. That is a day's walk. But she could have. If you need to go to Chivhu to look for her family, Babamukuru will take you in the car. It is too long a journey to walk.'

'That is kind, Tete Precious, very kind. But Chivhu is a big place and I don't know if we will have any luck finding her relatives amongst all those people. It is a long way to go to find nothing. I think we should wait and see. I am sure her family will come and look for her soon.'

Tete Precious looked doubtful but nodded.

'Thank you both. But now see, it is late. The stars are singing for us to go to bed,' Amai said.

'Come around tomorrow morning, Amai. We will discuss this matter further.'

'Yes, I will. Thank you, Tete Precious.'

I looked back towards Tendai's hut before we left the compound. She was staring out at me from behind the door with huge eyes.

Chipo

I was happy to see Amai and Baba's compound again. At least it was a place that I recognized. Everywhere else was so unfamiliar.

Amai and Baba began to make preparations for bed. Amai laid out a reed mat for me next to hers in her hut. I lay down on it and Amai folded a blanket over me, which I snuggled into. Darkness had spread across the hut and I could just make out the giant shape of Amai huddled over me.

'There there, mwana. Don't worry. We will find your family. But in the meantime, you are safe with us. We will take care of you,' Amai said. 'I am going to talk to Baba outside. Then I will come to bed. I will not be long. Try to sleep, little mwana.' Amai patted my head.

I watched her shuffle outside and turned my head to stare up at the splintered shadows playing across the beams beneath the thatched roof. I listened to Amai and Baba talking in low voices.

'I fear the worst, Baba. This mwana has been abandoned by her mother. She comes from a poor family. You can see that from that skirt she was wearing, her messy hair. This little girl's mother must have been penniless and desperate. She needed our help. She has left her mwana with us because she knows we will look after her well. And now the mwana doesn't speak because she is suffering from sadness. She knows that her mother has left her and so she has become mute with grief.'

'I think you are right, Amai. But why us? Whoever left her

with you today must have known that we have wanted children for many years and have never been blessed with a child. That is why her mother left her with us rather than the other neighbours with their big families. That means her mother must know us, so she must be from a nearby village.'

'That is true, Baba. She must come from close by. But wherever she is from, if her mother has left this mwana with us, then it is a blessing. We were chosen because we can give her proper care. We don't have any children, we have always wanted children, and here the ancestral spirits have given us a mwana! We should be rejoicing!'

'It doesn't work like that, Amai. There is more to this story.'

'Listen to me, Baba, we don't know the full story now, but I am sure it will become clear. News will come to us. We will discover in time. But until then, she is in our care.'

'Yes, that is true. We do not have any choice in this matter. We must look after this little girl until her mother comes to collect her.'

'So you agree, Baba? We will keep her?'

'Yes. We will keep her for the time being.'

'Pururururrruuuu!' Amai ululated joyfully. I heard her clapping her hands and dancing around. I shuffled away from the reed mat and poked my head around the hut door to watch her. She noticed my head peeping out, ran towards me and grasped my face in her hands. 'Pururururu!' she smiled down at me. For the first time today, I felt happy. Laughter gurgled in my throat. Amai looked at me astonished.

'See! You can cry, you can shout and you can laugh! All we need now is a few words. All in good time, isn't it, mwana.'

Amai laughed and swung my hands in hers as I huddled at the door of the hut. Baba interrupted our little dance.

'What shall we call her, while we wait for her mother to come back, Amai? We can't keep calling her 'mwana'.'

Amai looked at Baba with surprise. 'Ah, this little mwana, she already has a name, Baba! Her name is Chipo! Gift! She is a gift!'

Baba stood up and patted my head.

'Chipo,' he said. 'That is good. And now I am going to bed. It is late and we must be up early tomorrow.'

Baba made his way to his hut and Amai came to bed next to me. I was happy to have her there. I didn't want to be alone.

'You see, Chipo. Everything will be all right.'

A Sleepless Night

I awoke with the muddy feeling of not knowing who or where I was. Then I realized that this was true. No memories had swum back into my head during the night. I peeped my head around the door. Amai was stoking the fire and stirring a pot of sadza porridge outside the kitchen. There was a big tin pot of tea too, which Baba was pouring into three tin cups. I watched him ladle two spoons of sugar and two spoons of powdered milk into each. He walked over and handed me a cup, patting my head as I took it and sipped. It was delicious. The sweet liquid slipped down my throat and settled warmly in my stomach.

Morning had just unfurled and was stretching across the sky with a giant yawn. There was a pinch of chill in the air. I ventured outside to sit nearer the warmth of the fire and Amai handed me a plate of steaming sadza porridge.

'Did you sleep well, Chipo?'

I looked at her, sliding my new name around my head and trying to fit it in somewhere.

And then, with a start, I realised that I had hardly slept at all.

I had woken up in the middle of the night to the sound of a child wailing. It was as if it was inside the hut with Amai and me, right next to where we were sleeping. I had opened my eyes to see who was crying, but I didn't see anything. It was too dark, so dark that I couldn't even see the shadow of the door or the shape of the thatch above me. It was then that I realized that my toe, the one that the snake had flicked with its tongue was throbbing with acute pain. It was as if the snake had actually bitten my toe, and agony wrenched it with each scream that tore through the small hut. I had opened my eyes as wide as I could, staring hard into the night. The crying continued, getting louder. Correspondingly, the pain in my toe became almost unbearable. The wailing was so loud that I thought surely Amai would wake up. I tried to call out, 'who is there?' before remembering that my voice was trapped under my tongue, so I just lay there, listening and blinking into the night, gripping my throbbing toe in my hands to try and soothe it.

Eventually the wailing stopped. It shrunk to a whimper, and then a whisper, and then a gasp and then silence had flooded the hut, punctuated now and again by Amai's quiet snores. The pain slid out of my foot and into the earth, for I didn't feel it once the crying stopped. I had stayed awake, waiting for the child to start crying again. Finally, the rosy fingers of dawn started to pry open the lid of night and I had tumbled into a dreamless sleep.

Amai was watching me, waiting for my response. From her blank expression, I supposed that she hadn't heard the wailing.

I smiled and nodded.

'That is good. You need your sleep.' Amai took a hearty sip of tea.

My New Best Friend

'Today, we are going to get you something to wear, Chipo.'

I was rinsing the pots, plates and spoons with Amai behind the hut. The chickens were pecking at the leftovers that we had scraped off onto the earth. Baba had left for the day to tend to the maize crop.

'You are smaller than Tendai and I know that Tete Precious will be happy to give us something to keep you going, at least until we can go to the market to buy a dress. I also want to talk to Tete Precious. She is a wise woman. She will help us.'

We set off for Tete Precious's compound. The pampas grass brushed against my legs. Watching carefully for the snake as I walked, I tried to make sense of the midnight crying and the unbearable pain in my toe. I wondered how they were related, and if the snake was really an ancestor. If it was, were the events last night a clue to the message it had for me? I hoped desperately that Tendai would be at the compound. The only glimmer of recognition that I had seen since I had arrived here was on her face, so she may have some answers. I was so full of questions that my head was about to burst like a ripe marula fruit.

We arrived at Tete Precious's compound and my heart nearly leapt up into the sky when I saw Tendai there, busily sweeping around the smouldering fire. Her younger sister, the one with the limp that I had seen the night before, was watching her from an upturned wooden crate. The other children were playing with a lizard nearby, their shrieks and squabbles pealing like birds across the compound.

'Mangwanani, Amai.' Tete Precious and Amai clapped their greetings before Tete Precious turned to me.

'Eeeh! You are lucky it is school holidays, little one. Tendai is here! She can show you around while I talk to Amai.'

'We are calling her Chipo while she is with us. She is a gift after all!' said Amai proudly.

'Yes, that is a good name. Hello Chipo,' Tete Precious clapped her greeting to me and I clapped my hands to return it.

Tendai had stopped sweeping to listen. I left Amai and Tete Precious to their discussion and walked towards her.

'Hello, Chipo,' she said, a smile stretched across her face. I was surprised. It was as if we were good friends, not the complete strangers we had been the night before. She scooped my arm up in hers.

'Come, let's get away from here. Let's go to the secret hiding place so we can talk.' Tendai rolled her eyes in the direction of her brothers and sisters who had caught the lizard and were now playing with it.

She squeezed her little sister's hand as we went past.

'Can I come too?' the little girl begged, struggling to her feet and limping after us.

'Not this time, Tandi. Chipo and I need to talk alone. We'll be back soon, though,' Tendai said gently.

Disappointed, Tandi lowered herself back onto the wooden crate. My heart butterflied with anticipation.

Sky Reading

Tendai led me through the bush away from the compound until we reached a clearing surrounded by dusty scrub and spindly, young msasa trees. The shrieks of the compound faded away.

'Come, sit here.' Tendai sat on the earth and patted the ground beside her. I lowered myself onto the dust. She grinned at me, her wide eyes sparkling with the reflection of the blue makeshift dress I was wearing.

'Now that we are away from everyone, you can tell me, Tsoko. Why are you here? What happened? I couldn't believe it when I saw you here last night. With grownups! I hope I did the right thing by pretending not to know you.'

I stared at her with disbelief. So she did know me — my real name must be Tsoko. But I didn't recognize her at all. I stared hard at her face, trying to spark some memory. Who was she? And why *had* she pretended not to know me? Questions pressed into my mouth like falling dominoes.

'NnnnGGGHHHHHHHH!' My tongue refused to move.

'So it's true? You really can't speak? I thought you were just pretending so you didn't have to explain who you were to Amai. I thought that if we got away from the grownups, we could talk. Can you say anything?'

Miserably, I shook my head.

She looked at me quizzically. 'What has happened to you, Tsoko?'

I scratched at my head and shrugged my shoulders.

'You don't know? Have you lost your memory?'

I nodded eagerly, relieved that she could decipher my gestures so well. Then I pointed to her and shrugged.

'What?' she blinked wildly. 'You mean, you don't remember me?'

I shook my head.

'You don't know even know who I am?' she whispered, her eyes growing wide. 'Why has this happened? Do you remember Llali? Or Pungwe?'

I dug desperately around inside my head. Llali? Pungwe? I could remember no such names. Were they my parents?

I shook my head again. Tears of frustration prickled behind my eyes.

Tendai turned to watch a troop of shiny, black ants winding past us on the ground. Then a grin dawned on her face as she grabbed a stick from the ground beside her.

'Here, I have an idea.' She handed me the stick. 'Write in the dust, here. Write anything. Write Tsoko'.

I took the stick and wrote as she had told me. The word 'Tsoko' unravelled in the dust like a ribbon.

'Ah! So you haven't forgotten everything. You remember the basics: how to breathe, how to walk, and how to write.'

And how to eat, I thought to myself. I nodded eagerly, grateful that Tendai was helping me find some answers.

'Come; let's move away from the tree. I have another idea,' she said. She beckoned me towards the middle of the clearing. 'Now, lie back with me, like this,' Tendai lay on her back in a kite-shape of sunlight, looking up at the sky. She put her arm out for me to rest my head on. I lay next to her and gazed up into the steep blue. It went on forever and ever, beyond my lost memories, beyond Zimbabwe, beyond everything.

'If you still remember the basics, then I'm sure this is going to work,' said Tendai. 'What do you see? Do you see any clouds?'

I stared up at the empty sky and shook my head.

'No? Look again. Look for the clouds.'

I squinted. The sky was as clear as crystal, the only thing in it was the giant, white sun. Tendai was peering at me intently like a chameleon, her stare burning into the side of my face. I felt self-conscious and was about to shake my head when, suddenly, I felt

23

the familiar swirling feeling in my stomach again. As I stared up into the sky, the feeling expanded and spread up my body, into my throat and my head as it had done the night before. And then the sound of rushing air filled my ears.

Tendai peered closer at me and laughed. 'Ah, something's happening! I can tell. I knew this would work. Now concentrate, Chipo. Look for the clouds.'

I couldn't see anything apart from an empty blue. But I could feel this familiar floating feeling, as familiar as breathing, or eating, or writing. I allowed the swirling sky feeling to swallow me completely. I forgot Tendai, I forgot Amai, I forgot the compound, and then I saw it. It was a wisp of cloud so faint that it looked as if it would melt into the sky.

'Concentrate! Look for Pungwe!' Tendai's voice seemed far, far away.

I squinted hard as the wispy cloud bloomed into definition. It was like watching a tiny tadpole become a frog. And then, with a shock, I realized what it was. The cloud was a small boy. I gasped with surprise. It was a strange looking boy with a giant head and a small, stocky body, but it was a boy nonetheless. He looked like a toddler with giant, saucer eyes. I could see him in perfect detail, from his chubby fingers to his round belly punctuated in the middle with a belly button. He had a strange gaping hole in his forehead.

Like a mealie corn popping in a

hot pan, the name came to me. Pungwe. This was Pungwe. So Pungwe was a child. Was he my brother? I pulled my concentration away from the sky and looked at Tendai who was still watching me carefully, her lips pulled back in an excited smile.

'You've seen something! What did you see?'

With the stick, I drew a rough figure of a little boy in the dust.

'Pungwe! You saw Pungwe!'

I nodded, grinning happily. At last, this was something that made sense. It was a clue to who I was. Hope spilled into me.

'I knew it! I knew you would be able to do this. Now listen. See if he has anything to say to you.'

I returned my gaze to the sky. The sky feeling swirled through my body again and sound of rushing wind filled my ears. I squinted, peering up at the little cloud boy, and listened as hard as I could through the rushing wind. Suddenly it came flooding into my ears. It started off as a gasp, and then a whisper, and then a whimper and then a deep wailing. It was the same crying baby that I had heard the night before in Amai's hut, although now it was even louder. It was so loud that I thought my eardrums would burst. It filled my ears like water. I could just make out the words, 'She's ruined everything,' repeated again and again like waves. Once again, as if in reaction to the noise, pain erupted through my toe like a volcano, leaking agony out across my foot. It was so loud and so painful that I felt sick. I squeezed my eyes shut and put my hands over my ears.

Tendai gripped my arms and gave me a shake.

'I'm here!' she shouted. I opened my eyes and focused on her face. I slowly took my hands away from my ears. The wailing had stopped, the pain had retreated.

'Did he say anything to you?' Tendai asked.

I nodded. With the stick, I wrote in the earth what I had heard.

'How strange. What does that mean? 'She' must be Lali, but what did she ruin?'

25

I dropped my head into my hands. Tendai put her arm around my shoulder and gave me a comforting squeeze.

'You need to look in the sky again. The sky will tell you the truth.'

I shook my head. I still felt nauseous from Pungwe's loud crying and didn't want to risk seeing him again.

'You don't need to see Pungwe if you don't want to. All you need to do is to ask the sky to show you what happened before you came here.'

If the sky had shown me Pungwe, then I guessed it must be able to show me other things. I had no choice but to trust Tendai.

'Come, lie back down. Put your head on my arm,' Tendai nodded encouragingly.

I lay back down with my eyes closed.

'Now, all you have to do is keep your question in your mind, and the sky will answer you.'

I opened my eyes and stared up into the sky again. The swirling feeling quickly filled my body, and I asked over and over again in my head, 'Please, show me what happened before I came here.'

I was ready to snap my eyes shut at the first sight of Pungwe, but he didn't appear. Instead, the clouds unfurled into a scene of an old woman huddled over a sleeping girl. I started. The little girl was me. I could tell because she was wearing the same rabbit-skin skirt that I was wearing when Amai found me. I peered closer into the clouds, still repeating the question in my mind. The swirling sensation grew stronger in me as I focused.

The old woman seemed to be crying. She was muttering something, but I couldn't quite make it out. Her quiet mumbles were lost in the sound of rushing air. She had something in her hand. It looked like a small bowl. As the girl, I, slept, the old woman took something from the bowl and slipped it into the girl's mouth. A sharp taste slid over my tongue as I watched, and I nearly wretched. It tasted acrid, like blackened meat. Then the old woman took something from a pouch around her neck and wiped something across the girl's forehead. I could feel it on my head now. A freezing cold sensation seeped through my skin and into my mind, and suddenly everything went black.

'Tsoko! Tsoko, wake up!' Tendai was shaking me vigorously. I opened my eyes and blinked. The sky behind her was clear again, the clouds had disappeared. 'You fell asleep, Tsoko!'

I rubbed my eyes, and then remembering what I had seen in the dream, I jumped up and grabbed the stick. In the dust, I wrote 'MUTI'. Magic medicine. That is what the old woman had given me. She had made me eat something bitter to take away my voice, and then she had rubbed something icy cold across my forehead to make me forget everything. At least that explained why I couldn't speak, and why I had forgotten who I was.

But who was that old woman? She must have been a sangoma, a witch doctor. Only a witch doctor could have given me muti.

Tendai interrupted my thoughts. 'But why would Llali give you this muti? Why would she want to take away your memory and voice?'

That was Llali? My mother was a witch doctor?

'Don't worry, Tsoko. We will get to the bottom of this. I am your shamwari, your best friend, and if your shamwari can't help you, I don't know who can.'

I looked at her again, my eyes wide. My shamwari? That would mean that I came from close by. Baba had said that last night too. If my home was nearby, I would be able to return soon. And more importantly, it would be easier to uncover the truth about why Llali had given me the muti, and why Pungwe was so upset.

'Do you know what we need to do? We need to go and see Llali herself to ask her.'

My heart leapt. Tendai must know where I lived. Of course she did, if we were shamwaris. I wondered if we could go there now. I jumped up and pulled Tendai after me.

'There is only one problem,' said Tendai, jumping up with me and then lowering herself down to the ground. 'Llali lives near Chivhu, one day's walk away. And you have forgotten how to get back there.'

I blinked with confusion. If my mother lived one day's walk away, how did I know Tendai? How could I have met her before if I lived so far from here? It did explain why no one in this village knew me, though.

Questions rolled like dung beetles around my head. I thought Tendai would answer my questions, not give me even more.

I started to write one of them in the dust with the stick. 'If I come from Chivhu, how...' Tete Precious's voice broke through the bush and entered the clearing, calling for us. I scrawled the remainder of the question, '...do I know you?'

Tete Precious called our names again.

'We'd better go,' Tendai said. 'That question is going to take a while to answer. I'll tell you when we have more time.' She squeezed my hand. 'We will find out what has happened to you.

Don't worry, shamwari,' she said.

We brushed the dust off our clothes and made our way back through the scrub towards the compound.

Nearly Thirteen

'Look!' Amai shouted to us as we appeared through the trees. 'Tete Precious has kindly offered you these two dresses, Chipo! They used to be Tendai's but she has grown out of them, and you are smaller than her. There are plenty more for Tandi and the others. You can wear one now. That blue headscarf is not an ideal dress and I need it back to wear on my head!'

I untied the blue headscarf from under my arms and slipped a short-sleeved orange dress over my head. It was sun-bleached with a faded floral pattern. Now my shoulders were covered as well as my body. It felt strange to not feel the sun on my skin, the air on my back. Surely, I must have been used to wearing clothes before ... but then again, if my mother was a witch doctor, maybe not.

'Tendai is getting big so quickly, isn't she, Amai? Look at her! Before you know it, she will outgrow all her dresses. She will be thirteen very soon!' Tendai looked embarrassed. Then Tete Precious turned to me. 'I wonder how old you are Chipo? You must be nine or ten?'

'No, she is my age. She is twelve,' Tendai said. Then, realizing that she had slipped up, she cast her eyes quickly to the ground.

'How do you know this, Tendai?' Tete Precious and Amai asked simultaneously, their eyes wide.

Tendai quickly recovered and said, 'because she is more like me than Tandi. Tandi is only nine, but Chipo acts more like my age.'

Tete Precious and Amai laughed. 'You children!'

29

I exchanged a glance with Tendai. She grinned at me.

I hoped that Amai and Tete Precious would carry on talking so Tendai and I could continue our discussion, but Amai heaved herself off her little stool and held out her hand to me.

'Come, Chipo. We have things to do. We must go to the river to collect water. How good it will be to have a little helper! And we can bathe while we are there. You will be going to the river this morning, won't you, Tete Precious? We will see you there later.'

Amai turned to me. 'I'm glad you've made a new friend, Chipo.'

She beamed at Tendai, and Tendai gave me a conspiratorial smile.

A Surprise in the Water

We returned to the compound to collect the buckets and continued down the hill towards the river. I followed Amai along a dusty track edged with dry, sand-coloured pampas. Amai was singing a bird song, 'Shiri yakanaka, unoendepi? Pretty bird, where do you come from?' as we walked.

My thoughts buzzed like bees around the snake, the boy in the clouds, and my mother, the witch doctor with her strange, bitter muti. I wondered why she would do this to her daughter. What had happened? I kept stealing glances at the bright, blue sky. Whenever I did, the familiar sky feeling stirred in my belly and I felt comforted.

The pampas became greener as we neared the river. We walked along the lush path until we came to a large, smooth rock on the riverbank that sloped gently into the water. It was busy with mothers and their children sitting the heat. Some were dipping their feet in the water, some were swimming and others were lounging further up the rock in the drowsy sun.

'Off you go!' said Amai, putting the buckets down and settling

herself on the rock in a patch of shade. 'Don't go too far in the water, Chipo. There are crocodiles in this river. There has only been one crocodile attack a long time ago, but it is better to be safe.'

I was relieved to wriggle out of the dress, which although I was grateful for it, was far too hot. I clambered down the sun-baked rock towards the river. The sun sparkled on the surface of the water like a million fireflies. I inched my way in until I was submerged up to my chin and then I lay on my back and let myself drift. Underwater secrets scuttled and coiled in my ears.

I felt as if I could fall asleep, drifting like a baby hippo in the gentle currents. My eyes were half closed when I felt a drop of water flick on my face. I lifted my head out of the water and saw that I had floated away from the rock, nearly into the middle of the river. I was further out than the other bathers. I looked over at Amai who was lying back on the rock. I could just about see that her eyes were closed.

Another splash hit me in the eye, and I looked around to see where it had come from. There was nothing around me. The sky was empty with no sign of rain. Remembering Amai's warning about the crocodiles, I started to swim closer to the rock. Suddenly something grabbed me from under my body with what felt like small, round, clubbed hands and pushed me up to the surface of the water, so my whole body was almost completely lifted out of the river. I gasped with shock. Before I could struggle free from whatever was gripping me, I found myself being propelled across the river towards the rock. It happened so fast that I had no time to panic.

Just before I reached the rock, whatever had grabbed me released its clutches and I sank back under the cool currents. I looked around me, blinking wildly. There was nothing. I looked towards the rock. Everyone was as they had been moments before. No one had even noticed. Amai was still snoozing.

And then I had an idea. I would ask the sky.

Pungwe

I wriggled myself up onto the rock so my legs were still in the water and gazed up at the bright blue. The sun was directly overhead, stark white in the empty sky. The familiar feeling swirled into my stomach and spread quickly through my body, filling my ears with the sound of wind. It seemed to happen faster the more I practised.

'What was that in the water?' I asked, again and again, waiting for the clouds to come. I squinted into the blue and the shape of Pungwe appeared. I was just about to snap my eyes shut before the screaming sound filled my ears again, before I realized that he was shaking with mirth. Laughter crackled through the air. The boy in the cloud stared down at me, cackling. Through the rushing wind, whispered words spilled into my ears.

'You should have seen your face!' the whisper sparked and cracked. 'Eeeesh! Tsoko, you were so shocked! That was me, stupid! It was me who pulled you across the river.'

A strangled cry of pain uttered from my throat. The pain in

my toe throbbed with each syllable that Pungwe spoke. It was as if the pain was directly linked to him, and it was so intense that it was practically impossible to concentrate on sky reading at the same time. With all of my concentration, I turned my attention away from the throbbing in my toe. The ache howled and screamed, but my attention carefully skirted it and returned to sky reading.

I stared up into the sky, stunned. So that was Pungwe who propelled me across the river? Did he have magic like our mother?

Pungwe continued, still sniggering. 'I am pleased to see that you have not forgotten your special talent, Tsoko. You still know how to read the sky. Eeesh, Llali's muti is so strong that you couldn't even remember your own name! But she could not make you forget to read the sky. That is your own gift. She can't take that away from you. That is good for me. I can easily teach you what you have forgotten. It will not take long. I will give you your memory back, just you wait and see. Llali is foolish for thinking she can meddle with my plans!' Cackling laughter rang through my ears again.

My heart was jumping in my chest like a cricket. There was something strange about the way he was speaking. He didn't sound like a little boy. His voice was scratched and brittle and his laughter sounded too grown up for a baby brother. And why did this intense pain pierce my toe whenever he spoke to me?

Pungwe stopped laughing and peered down at my suspicion with concern.

'Don't be scared, Tsoko. You don't ever need to be frightened of me. I am always with you, always looking after you. I have taken care of you since you were small. I will help you now.'

But Pungwe was my little brother, so how could he have taken care of me when I was small, before he was even born?

'Tsoko, you must trust me. I will take care of you. And now you need my help more than ever. You need to be careful in the water. There is a garwe, a big crocodile, on the other side of the river, Tsoko. He was watching you. You'd make a feast for a hungry croc. He was just waiting for you to drift a little closer to him and then he would have come in to get you. That is why I pulled you back to the rock. You are no match for a hungry garwe. Not like before.'

A chill shivered through me. I might have been the second crocodile incident in the village. But what did he mean, 'Not like before?'

'Eeesh, Tsoko, you really have forgotten everything. Before Llali gave you the muti to forget everything, you had strong Masaramusi magic. Llali taught you how to make magic muti, how to talk to animals, how to be invisible and how to fly like a bird. That is how you used to come here from Chivhu. You flew. And me, I taught you the most important lesson; how to escape garwes.' I winced as a blade of pain sliced up my leg.

My mind whirred with confusion. Magic? Talking to animals and becoming invisible? Knowing how to fly? And how could I ever have escaped a crocodile? No one can do that. It's impossible. I squinted up into the sunlight, bracing myself against the agony in my foot.

34

'Not impossible, Tsoko. True. Yes, Llali taught you Masaramusi, but now see, she has made you forget all of it. That is not a problem for me, I can help you remember it all. You used to be able to see me, but now you can't. You can still see me in the clouds, but you used to be able to see me in real life. Look, here I am. I am swimming just by your foot.'

I looked down at the painless foot floating in the water. The other was clutched tightly in my hand as I tried to squeeze the pain from it. There was nothing there. I squinted hard and concentrated, and could make out a faintly brown, wavery wateriness in the air. It was so slight, that it could be imagined, but I knew it was Pungwe. I wondered how Pungwe still had his magic and still knew how to be invisible. Had our mother not given him the same muti that she had given me? And what was this plan that Llali had ruined? Nevertheless, if Pungwe could help me fish the memories from the great lake of forgetfulness in my head, I was happy he was my friend.

A Memory

My thoughts were interrupted by a shout and laughter. Tete Precious, Tendai and the other children were ambling onto the rock towards Amai. Tendai was waving to me. She left Tete Precious, Amai and the others to clap their greetings and clambered down towards me. I released my foot. The intensity of the pain had completely vanished. I wriggled my toes. It was as if they had never felt the agony that had frozen them while I was talking to Pungwe.

As I watched her make her way down the rock, I noticed a girl sitting further up the rock. There was nothing extraordinary about her, except for her eyes. They were black and shiny, like obsidian marbles. She was watching me closely, her stare pierced through me, hypnotising me like a snake. I was still locked in her stare when Tendai arrived.

She followed the direction of my eyes.

'Ah, that is Sipo. I wonder why she is staring at you like that. She looks as if she knows you. Well, she *is* in our class at school, but...'

My eyes snapped back to Tendai's face. We went to school together? But I lived a day's walk away from here!

Reading my mind, Tendai laughed and said, 'There is so much I need to tell you! Yes, you came with me to school. You used to make yourself invisible and sit beside me. That is how you knew how to write when I gave you the stick this morning. We learnt together. But no one could see you, so I don't know why Sipo is looking at you like that.'

'You used to know how to disappear and become like the air. You always kept yourself a secret, so people wouldn't ask questions. Lali told you that whenever you were away from her compound in Chivhu, you should stay invisible. That's why I was so confused when I saw you with Amai last night. I couldn't believe that you had shown yourself to someone else, let alone a grown up.'

So what Pungwe had just told me was true. I used to know how to be invisible like him. I shook my head and smiled.

'But Sipo there,' Tendai's tone sank low, drawing my attention back to Snake Eyes, 'she looks strange, doesn't she? Her eyes are as black as a mamba's. I wonder what has happened to her?'

Goose pimples bristled up on my skin as I looked at Snake Eyes again.

'Have you had any more luck with the clouds?' Tendai's voice broke into my thoughts.

I grinned excitedly at Tendai and nodded.

'Good. I knew you would. You used to tell me about the stories you had seen in the clouds and they would always come true. It worked well in exams. You could read in the clouds what questions would come up, and they always would. That is how clever your sky reading was.'

I stared at her, my eyes round with disbelief. I couldn't believe she was talking about me. This all sounded like a dream. Tendai laughed at my confused expression.

'You wanted to know how we met. The first time I met you was around here, by that lucky bean tree.' Tendai pointed to a large, leafy tree on the riverbank near the edge of the rock.

I looked over at the tree and suddenly, as quick as a kingfisher wing, I was swept into a memory. My heart started beating so fast with excitement that I thought it would gallop out of my chest. It was so vivid, I could see, feel and hear everything so clearly. I was sitting in the lucky bean tree that Tendai had just pointed out. I felt safe and protected in the leafy branches. I held my hand up to my face, but instead of my flesh, there was a shimmery light that would have been imperceptible to anyone who wasn't looking for it. I was completely invisible. I looked down through the branches and saw a girl. She was collecting the lucky beans that had fallen to the earth. I wanted to join her but I knew I had to stay hidden. I shook the branches so more lucky beans would fall out for her to collect.

As I watched the bright red lucky beans falling, I heard a sharp hiss. My heart jumped into my throat. I knew that sound well. It was the sound of a boomslang. Boomslangs are notoriously cheeky snakes. They hide in the trees and wait for an animal to walk under them. When this happens, they drop from the branch onto their prey and bite them. Their venom is so deadly that, once bitten, the victim dies almost instantly. A boomslang is almost completely silent, which makes it all the more deadly. The only sound it makes is a loud, warning hiss as it falls through the air. This hiss is the only chance the victim has to escape.

I watched with horror as the boomslang's bright, green body  fell through the air towards the girl. Alerted to the hiss, she looked up. Her face was familiar, and in an instant, I recognised Tendai. She saw the snake falling towards her and jumped smartly out of the way. The boomslang landed on the ground by her feet. My heart froze. The boomslang would surely bite her foot and that would be the end of her.

I knew that I needed to stay invisible, that I could not be seen, but I didn't want her to die. And so I took a chance and sang my snake song. It was a strange sound, whispering and watery like wind over a clay pot. I watched the snake closely as I sang. It swung its head around and looked up at me through the branches. As I sung louder and louder, its eyes grew so big that I thought they would take over its whole head. Tendai was now peering up through the branches too, trying to see where the sound was coming from. Of course she couldn't see me, but she knew there was something there.

Finally, the snake turned away from her and slithered into the scrub. Tendai crumpled onto the ground and sobbed with relief. I made myself visible and clambered down the tree to comfort her.

'Mhoroi! Hello!' I said.

She looked up at me with bewilderment.

'Who are you?' She asked. 'And where did you come from just now?'

'I am Tsoko,' I said. 'And I came from the lucky bean tree.'

As quickly as it had swept me up, the memory vanished. I came to as if waking up from a dream. Tendai was watching my face.

'Are you remembering? Did you just have a memory?' she asked.

I nodded. I wished I could tell her that I remembered how we became friends.

Joy surged through me. My memories were still in my head. They were just locked away somewhere that I couldn't access at the moment. But I would.

The Tokoloshe

I looked around. The shade on the rock was shrinking as the sun climbed up the sky. Amai and Tete Precious were chatting contentedly. Tendai's brothers and sisters were splashing each other and Tandi was playing by herself in the shallow water. Snake Eyes was still watching me intently. I shivered and turned back to Tendai.

'I want to show you something,' Tendai said, jumping up.

I followed her towards the lucky bean tree.

'Do you think you can remember to climb?' she asked.

I nodded.

Tendai climbed quickly. Her feet knew all the knots and ledges. I followed her carefully, putting my feet where her feet had been and using the same handgrips she used. She stopped at the top of the trunk where the branches split out in different directions. There was a hollow in the centre of these branches, which was big enough for us both to sit in. I clambered up after her. It was the same place that I was sitting in my memory.

An excited grin spread across Tendai's face as she reached her hand into a small hole in one of the branches. I thought nervously about the boomslang that had fallen from this same tree. Pungwe's warning rang through my head; I didn't have my magic anymore. I no longer knew how to sing to snakes and I couldn't protect either of us as I used to. I hoped Tendai realized this too. She didn't pull out a boomslang, though. She pulled out a handful of necklaces. My mouth fell open with surprise. There were necklaces made from lucky beans, necklaces made from bird feathers, necklaces made from small bones. I reached out to take the one that caught my eye. It was made from thousands of yellow, jagged teeth. My fingers closed around the sharp edges.

'That one is made from crocodile's teeth. It is to protect you from the crocodiles in this river. It is a Tokoloshe necklace. Pungwe gave it to you.'

My eyes bulged when she said this. I wrote a 'T' on the palm of my hand with my finger and looked at her with terror. Tendai laughed.

'Did you not know that Pungwe was a Tokoloshe?'

I quickly shook my head. Although his voice had sounded brittle, unlike that of a little brother, it had never crossed my mind that Pungwe was anything but human.

There is no creature more terrifying than a Tokoloshe.

Slave to the N'anga, the bad wizard, a Tokoloshe is responsible for carrying out the N'anga's evil deeds. Every living creature fears it. Whenever there is a death in the village, everyone knows that a Tokoloshe is behind it. If there is an outbreak of cholera, it was the Tokoloshe who brought the disease to the village and spilled it across the land. And more terrifying still, a Tokoloshe can get away with murder as it is invisible to human eyes.

'Yes, Pungwe is a Tokoloshe. When you saw him in the clouds, didn't you see the hole in his head from where the N'anga created him? Didn't that tell you that he was a Tokoloshe?' Tendai responded to my confusion.

I remembered the gaping hole in Pungwe's forehead. How could I not have suspected anything? Folklore says that in order to create a Tokoloshe, the N'anga must drive a human bone sharpened to a spike into the head of a human corpse. The corpse then shrinks to half its size, all goodness flows out of the hole in its head and it becomes a Tokoloshe, immortally cursed. The only corpses that are safe from the fate of being made into a Tokoloshe are those of children. Tokoloshes can only be created from people older than thirteen.

Tendai laughed at my horrified expression.

'Don't worry, Tsoko. Pungwe is not bad like the other Tokoloshes. He worked for the evil N'anga during nights and came to find you during the day. That N'anga is a bad man. He uses very dark magic, and Pungwe hates him. Pungwe says that there is so much work to do and he struggles to finish it all. No matter how hard he tries, the N'anga punishes him.'

I studied the crocodile tooth necklace. If Pungwe was a Tokoloshe, how could Tendai see him? She read my thoughts again.

'I never saw Pungwe. You would tell me when he was there, and what he was saying. You and Pungwe used to try to teach me tricks like how to be invisible and how to make ants fly, but it didn't work with me. You have a natural magic in you.'

I wrote an 'L' on my palm with my finger and looked at her questioningly.

'L… You mean Llali?'

I nodded.

'Llali found you when you were a baby. She said that you were given to her as a gift. She was barren and childless when you came to her, and she loved you as her own. She is very old, the Sangoma, maybe even older than an ambuya elephant. She taught you all her magic so when she dies, her magic will not die with her. And she is very kind. Her magic is good.'

So Llali was not my real mother. And whatever had happened must have been serious. By abandoning me, she was alone again and her magic would be lost when she died anyway.

I held up the necklace made from small bones and looked at Tendai questioningly. It had a sinister feeling to it.

'Ah, that one is a dangerous one,' Tendai said, shaking her head. She snatched it away from me and stuffed it back in the hole. 'Pungwe gave it to you. I think he stole it from the N'anga. That necklace curses people so they have bad luck for their whole lives. Their families die from terrible diseases, their homes burn down, they have to live in the bush with the animals, they die alone and their bodies are eaten by hyenas. You never used it. Llali warned you against bad magic. She said that any magic you made would come back to you, so if you used bad magic, you would curse your own life.'

A sick feeling unfurled in my stomach. I wanted to take that necklace out of the hole and bury it so no one could find it. I held up the lucky bean necklaces to change the subject. There were four of them.

'These are the good ones. They bring luck and happiness to whoever wears them. We both used to wear them all the time. They are from Llali, a gift.'

I admired them. The beans were bright, shiny red with a black dot like an eye on each. They were threaded closely together and made a satisfying clicking sound when they knocked against each other. I put two around my neck and gave the other two to Tendai.

'I hope they still work. Now that you don't have your magic, I think we need some luck to help us solve this mystery,' she grinned.

The Crocodile

The sound of a twig snapping below us broke Tendai's grin. I looked down through the branches to see what had made the sound and gasped. It was Snake Eyes. She peered up at me, her stare burrowing under my skin. Tendai leaned over to see what I was looking at. For a second, no one said anything.

Then Tendai shouted down:

'What are you doing there, Sipo? What do you want?'

Snake Eyes continued to stare up at us. My heart was beating wildly in my chest. It felt as if it might burst out of me and flutter away.

'Come down. I need to talk to you,' she said. Her voice was shaky, as if she was worried about something.

'What are you talking about? We don't need to come down there to hear you. Sipo, tell us what you want. And what has happened to your eyes? You look strange!' Tendai shouted through the branches.

'Please, come down. I have something to tell you,' she said. Her face was etched with anxiety.

Tendai and I exchanged a look.

Suddenly a cry broke through the silence between us. It was coming from the rock. Snake Eyes snapped her black eyes away from us and sped off to where the commotion was coming from. I looked at Tendai. Her face had dropped in horror.

'Tandi! That was Tandi's voice!' she whispered as she started grappling her way down the tree. I grabbed the crocodile tooth necklace and slung it over my head before I followed her. We scooted quickly down the branches. The teeth clicked angrily against the lucky bean necklaces. I followed Tendai as precisely as I could, but kept slipping.

'Come ON!' Tendai yelled at me from the ground. I slipped on the last branch and fell the last part of the way, landing hard. Tendai grabbed my hand to pull me up and we raced towards the river. The cries were getting louder and I could distinguish Tete Precious's screams. My heart quickened in my chest as I chased Tendai through the bushes towards the rock.

When we arrived, my heart jumped into my mouth. A crocodile was grappling with something in the water close to the edge of the rock.

'TANDI!' Tete Precious was screaming hysterically. I looked around me. Tandi had disappeared from the rock. I looked at the crocodile. It had Tandi between its jaws. She was screaming in terror as the crocodile snapped its teeth around her. It must have been the same crocodile from the other side of the river that Pungwe had rescued me from.

Instinctively, I knew what to do. I raced towards the water. Tete Precious and Amai stopped screaming for Tandi and were now screaming at me to stop. My hand gripped the crocodile tooth necklace around my neck. An incredible strength pulsed through my fingers. The crocodile was trying to wrestle Tandi away from the rock. Its jaws had closed around her leg and it was shaking her in all directions like a rag. I lunged towards them through the water, strength surging through me like a bonfire.

As I thrashed my way towards it, the crocodile whipped its head around to confront whatever had dared to interrupt its hunt. Tandi's leg was still jammed in its jaws. She had grown limp; her eyes were wide with terror. The water was red and bloody. The crocodile let out a cough of frustration as I thrashed closer and closer. It opened its jaws wide to scare me away, exposing rows of yellow teeth. As it did this, Tandi rolled out of its mouth and floated face down in the red water. The crocodile hesitated. I was so close now that I could see the tough, gnarled patterns on its skin. With another angry cough, the crocodile retreated and wriggled its way through the currents and away from us.

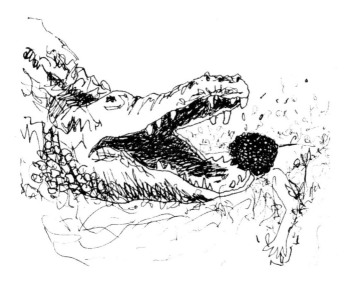

Silence dropped like a stone. The screaming that had been pealing through the air moments ago collapsed. I grabbed Tandi. She flopped in my arms. She was panting like a wounded gazelle, her eyes wide and unblinking. The water was shallow enough to pull her easily out of the river and onto the rock. Blood was pouring from her leg. It pooled, watery and bright, around her before trickling down into the water.

Chipo the Hero

A crowd of spectators pressed closely as I stroked poor Tandi's stricken forehead.

'Tandi!' Tete Precious was distraught. Her face was pulled into a tight grimace. She elbowed her way through the crowd towards her daughter. She grabbed Tandi's broken body and scrambled up the rock, shouting for help.

'Get Babamukuru!' she shouted. 'We need the car! We need to get Tandi to the clinic! Quickly! Go to the fields! Get

Babamukuru!'

Four of the younger children sprinted off over the rock in the direction of the fields.

I followed Tete Precious as she carried Tandi towards the compound. Tendai and Amai were moments behind me. Blood was pouring from Tandi's leg, tracing a thick, dark trail from the river to the compound on top of the hill. Once we were at the compound, Tete Precious laid Tandi down on a reed mat under the tree and fetched some fabric to tie around the wound as a bandage. Tears flooded her face as she secured it around Tandi's leg.

'How could I let this happen to poor Tandi? My poor, poor Tandi! It is my fault! I should have been watching her. I should have warned her sooner! With her limp, she can't run quickly enough to escape a crocodile! This is my fault.'

'It is not your fault, Tete Precious, not at all. But we need to think quickly. Are you taking her to the clinic? Will you make it there in time?' asked Amai.

Tete Precious froze.

'Maiwe! We will not make it in time! I did not think of this. The clinic is too far. It is at least seven hours by car. No, we will need to take her to Llali, the Sangoma in Chivhu instead. She is a good woman. She will be better than the clinic. And it is only three hours to get there if we drive quickly. That is where Babamukuru must drive us. Tandi will be all right for three hours if we keep her leg lifted.'

Tendai looked at me. Once again, we were thinking the same

thing. I needed to see the Sangoma too.

Tendai spoke up. 'Tete Precious, Chipo should go in the car too. She should come with you to the Sangoma. The Sangoma might be able to help with her voice. She might be able to tell us where Chipo is from and who her family is.'

At this suggestion, Tete Precious turned to me and stared at me as if I was an ancestral spirit come to life.

'Chipo! How can I have not said tatenda, thank you, to you? It is because of you that Tandi is still with us. I don't know why the crocodile ran away from you, but if you hadn't gone in after my daughter, she would be dead. Yes, you are a brave mwana. Or maybe you are just as stupid as an ostrich. I just don't know whether or not to chastise you for being so foolish or to love you for succeeding in your foolishness,' she gasped.

'I think we should be grateful, Tete Precious. Let's not think of the consequences. What happened, happened. Both Tandi and Chipo are all right. That is what is important. Our new daughter has already proven her worth. She has already lived up to her name,' said Amai.

There was silence as everyone turned to look at me, and Amai pulled me into a hug.

'Thank you, Chipo. You saved my Tandi, and for that, you are an honoured person in my home,' Tete Precious sobbed. 'Tendai is right. The Sangoma might be able to help you get your voice back. What do you say, Amai?'

'Eeesh, Tete Precious, I would be so grateful if you would take this little one with you. Whatever the Sangoma can do to help her, Baba and I would be grateful.'

'And we will pay, Amai. Whatever the cost of Chipo's treatment, we will pay for it. Chipo saved my child's life and so I want to help her however I can. It is the least I can do.'

The Journey to Chivhu

Babamukuru ran into the compound, his eyes wide and hair dishevelled. 'Where is she? Where is my Tandi? Come, let's get her into the car! Quickly! There is no time to waste!'

He ran towards Tandi who was still laid out on the reed mat. The blood from her leg was seeping like a flame lily into her bandage. He picked her up gently and carried her behind the compound where the rickety, blue Peugeot was parked.

'We are going to the Sangoma in Chivhu, Babamukuru. The clinic is too far and Tandi will not last the distance,' Tete Precious panted after them.

'Yes, I agree,' Babamukuru said, his voice thick and serious.

'And we are taking Chipo too. The Sangoma will give Chipo some muti for her voice.'

'If what I heard is true, that Chipo saved my daughter from the crocodile, then that is the least we can do,' he said as he loaded Tandi gently into the back seat of the car.

The Peugeot turned out of the village and onto the dusty road to Chivhu. I watched the world sliding past my windows; the sandy brown of the road, the empty landscapes peppered with lonely thorn trees, the jewel-blue sky. Silence filled the Peugeot as we drove. Tandi's head was cradled in my lap and I tried to keep her as still as possible as the car jumped over potholes and rocks. She was asleep, her mouth small with pain. Her breathing was shallow and light. She looked so fragile, poor little Tandi.

I closed my eyes and lay back against the car seat with the sun beaming lazily through the window. It was hot, but comfortably so. I felt exhausted. So much had happened. Before long, I drifted into a kaleidoscope of dreams; the village, the snake, Tendai, Pungwe, the crocodile, the necklaces. At the centre of it all, though, was Snake Eyes. 'Chengerai!' she was saying in a voice as cool and slippery as oil. 'Danger!'

The Witchdoctor

I awoke with a start as we were driving through the woods towards the Sangoma's compound. The atmosphere in the car was tense. Tete Precious turned to check on Tandi and me. Her face was grey with worry. Babamukuru was staring grimly ahead, his hands rooted to the steering wheel.

'We are nearly there,' said Tete Precious to no one in particular. Anxiety wrapped itself around my heart, not only for Tandi, but also for myself. Would I recognize the Sangoma? Would she take me back?

The compound was hidden in dense, green bush. It was marked by an arched gateway made from delicate animal bones and skins. At the top of the gateway was a tiny duiker skull. Its black, hollow eyes watched the Peugeot drive under it. There was a space to park the car beside the gateway, and a path that lead up to the compound where the Sangoma sat with her back

to us as we pulled in.

Babamukuru carefully cradled the half-conscious Tandi in his arms. He carried her over to the Sangoma and murmured a respectful greeting. The Sangoma turned around to face her visitors. I gasped, not only because it *was* the same old woman that I had seen in the clouds, but also because as she turned towards us, she revealed a bloody pile of dead hares that she was skinning. The meaty corpses lay piled on one side, dark blood oozing from them, and their hides lay on the other. She noticed me gawping at the dead hares.

'It gets cold in the evenings. I am making a rug. And hare meat is good to eat. Its blood can make you run faster than a cheetah.' Her tone was factual. She was pretending that she didn't know me. I studied her face, the memory of its ancient, wide-set eyes and thin lips flickering somewhere deep in the recesses of my mind. She avoided my gaze and heaved herself off the ground.

She led Babamukuru and Tandi into one of the huts. Tete Precious and I followed at a safe distance. Llali's skin was crisscrossed with a spider web of wrinkles. She wore a cloak made from animal skins sewn together with thick twine and her neck was hung with hundreds of necklaces. Some were made from sticks, feathers and leaves. Others were made from polished stones and carried small, leather pouches. One of those pouches held the ice-cold muti that she had used on me.

We were ushered into a square, thatched hut. Tete Precious clutched me to her as we watched from the door. There were dried herbs hanging from the ceiling and hundreds of clay pots and wooden boxes clustered around the edges. A small fire smouldered slowly in one corner of the room, and dead leaves were piled up in another. The Sangoma indicated for Babamukuru to lay Tandi on the skin rug that was stretched out in the centre of the hut. Once he had done this, she waved him away. He retreated to join us, huddled at the entrance. Murmuring under her breath, the Sangoma unravelled the fabric that Tete Precious had wrapped around Tandi's wound. The bandage was stiff with dried blood. I wretched when I saw the fresh wounds that lay open and oozing beneath.

The Sangoma's murmuring grew louder as she lit a bundle of sharp-smelling herbs from the fire in the corner. She waved it over Tandi's leg, spilling heavy smoke over the bloody gashes. She beckoned me towards her. At first, I tried to hide behind Tete Precious, but the Sangoma beckoned to me again. Tete Precious gently nudged me forward, saying, 'Don't worry, Chipo, we are here.'

I inched slowly towards the Sangoma, trying desperately not to breathe in the starchy smoke. She thrust the bouquet of burning herbs into my hand and indicated that I should hold it over Tandi's mutilated leg so the smoke continued to fall on it. The Sangoma then picked up a small, clay pot. She moved around the hut and gathered ingredients from the various pots and boxes. I shut my eyes as she poured in what looked like blood. She told me that it was crocodile blood. I recoiled.

'You cure a bite with the same thing that caused the harm. For a snakebite, the cure is venom from the snake. For a crocodile bite, it is blood from the crocodile.'

She continued mumbling as she stirred and mixed and poured and measured. Finally, she showed me the resulting mixture. It was a dark, red paste. She pulled a large leaf from the pile in the corner and scooped up some of the paste. I wretched. The stench of it

caught in my throat. The crocodile blood made it smell of rotting flesh. The Sangoma smirked at my reaction. She smeared the red paste directly onto the biggest gash on Tandi's leg. The wounded girl's eyes flew open and agony seared across her face. Her scream sliced through me. Tete Precious rushed forward to comfort her but Babamukuru held her back. 'Shhhh, Precious. Let the Sangoma do her work.'

Once the Sangoma finished applying the paste, Tandi's screams settled to a quiet whimper. Her face was gripped by a pained grimace. The Sangoma collected some more leaves from the pile and placed these on top of the pasted wounds so they were completely covered. She straightened out the dark, bloody fabric, which Tandi had come in with and placed it over the top of the leaves, bandaging her leg up neatly.

As soon as the bandage was on, Tandi's face relaxed and she fell asleep. Tete Precious, who was still being held back by Babamukuru, broke down into tears. The Sangoma took the bunch of cindering herbs from my hand and placed it beside Tandi's sleeping head. She motioned that I should go to Tete Precious and Babamukuru, which I did gladly.

'Sangoma, will our little one be ok? Please tell me, Sangoma. Will she live?' Tete Precious's voice was clotted with tears.

The Sangoma looked up. Her gold, tortoise eyes flickered on me for an instant before moving to Tete Precious.

'Yes.' The Sangoma's voice was gnarled. 'This little one will be fine. She is lucky. The ancestral spirits were looking out for her today. Her leg bone is not even broken. It is only the skin and flesh that have been damaged.'

Tete Precious broke down into tears again and Babamukuru put his arm around her. The Sangoma's gaze shifted to me once more. I looked down at my feet to avoid her eyes, suddenly shy.

'Can I?' Tete Precious moved slightly towards Tandi.

The Sangoma nodded. Tete Precious rushed towards her daughter. She knelt beside her and held her hand tightly. Tandi moaned quietly, but continued to sleep. Babamukuru went to stand by Tete Precious and placed a hand on her shoulder.

Llali tells the Truth

This was my chance. I looked shyly at the Sangoma. She was watching me closely. Her wrinkled lips stretched into a creased smile. She nodded to me and I made my way gingerly across the hut towards her.

'I wondered when I might see you again, Tsoko,' she said to me quietly.

I looked into her golden eyes. So I was right. This *was* Llali. Hope twinkled like a star. Maybe she would take me back now that I had found her again. Maybe she would return my memories and my voice.

A sadness flickered across her face before she said, 'Tsoko, you do not understand. Never think that I abandoned you. That is not true. I took care of you for many years, since you were a baby. You were like my own daughter. It breaks my heart but you must start a new life, now. My muti has worked and you have forgotten everything. That is as I had wished, but you cannot come back to live with me here, and I will not return your memories.'

I looked down at my feet as misery slid a cold hand around my heart.

'There, there, my Tsoko. But you haven't forgotten your sky reading. You have always been able to do that. When you were a baby, before you could even talk, your eyes were always turned to the sky.'

My breath stopped in my throat as I struggled to keep from crying.

'You have met Pungwe again. And you are still wearing his necklace.' She fingered the crocodile tooth necklace with her shrivelled hand, her face set in a stern grimace. She dropped the necklace back to my chest with a sigh.

'Listen to me, Tsoko,' Llali's voice quickened as she held up her finger in warning. 'Pungwe is a Tokoloshe. There is no such thing as a good Tokoloshe. And this one is bad. Very bad. Do not trust him. He is very clever. He pretends to help you so you trust him. Tsoko, a Tokoloshe is the N'anga's slave. He works only for the N'anga, no one else. And if it is the bad N'anga from Chivhu, then this is a particularly nasty Tokoloshe.'

Why is he interested in me, then? What is this plan he keeps talking about? I wanted to scream.

Llali shook her tortoise head. She looked at me deeply, reading my thoughts.

'That is not important for you to know now, Tsoko. What is important is that Pungwe tricked you. You did not realize because you are young, naïve. You trusted him, loved him as your brother. If only I had found out sooner. I brought you into such a dangerous world with the magic I taught you and I didn't even know it. I only realized when you came home one day wearing that garwe necklace.'

My hand moved towards the crocodile tooth necklace.

'Yes, that is the one, Tsoko. You came home and you were wearing a necklace like that one. It is a Tokoloshe necklace. And then I knew that a Tokoloshe had befriended you. I asked you again and again, but you didn't want to say anything. Pungwe had made you promise never to tell me that you were friends with him because I would know what he was up to. Eventually you told me about him, though. You told me about the magic he had taught you and I knew then that you were in terrible danger. 'You must listen to me. I am very old and I am also very wise. I have done the best thing I could have done for you. I gave you some muti to make you forget everything. I wanted you to forget Pungwe, to be safe from him. I took away your magic so you would not be able to see him, and I took away your voice so you would not be able to speak to him. I had to act quickly, and that was the only way I could think of saving you. But I see that it has only partly worked. He has found a way of reaching you through the clouds. He wants to teach you magic again, doesn't he? He wants you to relearn what you have forgotten. Tsoko, if only you knew his plan. But it is not important. You have a new life now, and Pungwe will not be a part of it.'

Llali smiled weakly. 'But of course you want your voice back, Tsoko. You want to be able to tell your cloud stories again. You want to talk to Amai and Baba around the fire. You want to talk to Tendai.'

I nodded eagerly.

'Then I will give you your voice, but on one condition. You must not talk to Pungwe ever again. No matter how much he promises to teach you magic, or to give you back your memories, you must not speak to him.'

My breath stopped in my throat as I looked down to avoid her eyes. My brain felt like a jumbled Monkey Puzzle tree. I wished I knew what Pungwe's plan was. And how would I ever find out if Llali wasn't going to tell me, and if I couldn't talk to him. Pungwe had promised to help me recollect my memories. He had said he was going to teach me magic again. And he protected me from the crocodile. Surely that was good?

Llali laughed scratchily, once again reading my thoughts as easily as reading msasa leaves. Then her voice became hard as her eyes stared flintily into mine.

'Do you know what I will do, Tsoko, if you talk to the Tokoloshe again? I will give you some more muti so you will not only lose your tongue but you will lose your eyes as well. You are making an oath with me. You must never talk to Pungwe.'

I looked at her in disbelief. Tears pressed behind my eyes. How could this woman have brought me up as her own daughter? She was cruel. What kind of mother would abandon her daughter, would take away her memories, and make her mute, let alone blind?

'You are wrong there, Tsoko,' Llali said, reading my thoughts. 'A mother will do anything, absolutely anything, to protect her child. That is what I am doing for you. I am protecting you from Pungwe. I have no choice. And if that means I have to take away your words and your vision, and to live without my daughter while she is looked after by others, then so be it.'

I suddenly realized that the pain I felt in my toe whenever Pungwe was talking to me was because of Llali. She must have sent the snake to me with a spell. It was one more way she could save me from the Tokoloshe.

I sighed. There was no decision to make. Of course I wanted my voice.

'You have chosen wisely, my Tsoko. I knew you would. And it is time for you to be a normal girl. You should not have to worry about things like Tokoloshes. This muti will work overnight, so you should all stay here. You can leave tomorrow morning, and by then, you will have your voice. I have done my best for you, Tsoko. And I am always here if you need my help. But come; it is time for you to speak, Tsoko. And I must remember. Your name is Chipo now.'

Muti for a Voice

Llali approached Tete Precious and Babamukuru as they watched over Tandi. Although age had made the Sangoma stoop, she moved gracefully.

'I see that the other child cannot speak. I have some muti to help her.'

Tete Precious looked at me as if she had completely forgotten I was there. I felt a pang of envy. How lucky Tandi was to have parents who put her first above everything. They had completely forgotten about me.

'Of course! Of course, Sangoma! We had brought Chipo with us for that very reason. Forgive me for not saying anything sooner, it's just...' She nodded towards Tandi and Llali nodded kindly.

'Yes, that is your daughter. I understand. But I will help this other one, if you don't mind. It is very late. Too late to drive back with this sick one,' she gestured to Tandi. 'You should spend the night here and you can leave tomorrow morning. That is better for Chipo. Her muti will take one night's sleep to work.'

'Sangoma, that is very kind, but do you have room for us all to sleep? You are used to living alone here and there is not much room.'

'Of course, of course,' Llali waved their concerns away with a shrivelled hand. 'You will stay in this hut with Tandi. I have furs for you to sleep on. Chipo will stay with me. There is room in my hut for one other. I can watch over her during the night. But for now let's eat. It has been a long day.'

She dished us up with some left over hare stew and sadza, which we all ate greedily except for Tandi who was sound asleep. Tete Precious and Babamukuru nodded gratefully as Llali handed them some furs and helped them to lay them out on the ground.

'It is not much, I know, but it will see you through until morning,' Llali said.

Babamukuru and Tete Precious clapped their hands, bid us good night and returned their attention to Tandi.

The Spell

Llali motioned for me to follow her outside. Whilst we had been in the medicine hut, night had drawn its curtains against the day. I stayed close to Llali as she led me towards another square hut, similar to the previous one. As I entered, I wanted to cry. I recognised it. It felt like home.

'Yes, you are right, Chipo. This one was our hut. This is where we slept.'

I looked around. There was a large animal skin and a smaller one next to it, which would have been my bed.

'Yes, that was your rug,' Llali's voice wavered. She held my hand and said sadly, 'You have a new life now, Chipo; a normal life with normal people. It is your birthright.'

I nodded.

'Good girl. Now, you mustn't be scared, Chipo. This muti is simple and painless.'

Llali pulled out a long acacia thorn from a pouch around her neck. She told me to open my mouth and stick out my tongue. My first thought was that she was going to pierce my tongue with the thorn. I blinked rapidly and tried to pull away from her but she grabbed my arm. Suddenly I had changed my mind. I didn't want that thorn going through my tongue. I would rather be mute for the rest of my life. I pulled away from her

Llali chuckled.

'Silly girl. I am not going to hurt you. It will just be a small scratch. It is too late to change your mind. You have already made your decision. Hold out your tongue.'

Llali gripped my arm so hard that there was no escape. Shakily, I stuck out my tongue and squeezed my eyes shut against the pain. Once again, Llali started murmuring. I focused on the comforting rhythm of it, trying not to think about what she was doing with the thorn. I felt a little pressure on my tongue and then some drops of sweet liquid spilled across my taste buds. My

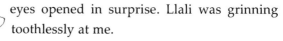

eyes opened in surprise. Llali was grinning toothlessly at me.

'You see, Chipo, it didn't hurt. I would not hurt you!'

'Nnnnggggghhhh!' I tried to speak but my voice didn't come. I shook my head in frustration.

'One night's sleep, Chipo. That's all it will take now. When you wake up tomorrow morning, you will have your words again. Come, let's sleep. You have had an exciting day.'

Kidnapped

It took a long time to drift off to sleep. Excitement about regaining my voice was thundering around my head like an elephant. That and the mixture of familiarity and strangeness of being in the hut with Llali overwhelmed my senses. My thoughts were cajoled and jostled by Llali's quiet snores as she sank deeper into her own dreams. I tossed and turned with frustration.

As I lay there, my eyes closed against the night, willing myself to sleep, something fell across my face. It was rough fabric, like a scrap of sack. A sudden, hot stink stung my nostrils and before I could jump up, I was fumbled by small, hoof-like hands into what felt like a large sack. It scratched against my legs and the stench of it was so fetid that I wretched.

'Nggnngngggghhhh!' I tried to shout, but of course my voice hadn't returned yet as I hadn't slept a full night. The same small hands pressed painfully into me, rolling me and sliding me along the floor. The rank, sulphurous stink of the sack, made me want to throw up. I recognized the small hoof-like hands from the river to be Pungwe. Not only that, but the familiar agony in my toe flared up again. Pungwe was grunting and groaning with the effort of heaving me across the floor. I struck out with my fist, hoping to hit him. In return, I received such a painful shower of blows to my head and back that my vision spun with stars for a moment while I recovered. I felt a smear of wet blood on the back of my neck and thought it better to succumb to his intentions quietly unless I wanted to be beaten to death.

I must have passed out from either the blow to my head or the stench of the sack, because the next thing I knew, I was back in fresh air, shivering and curled up against something soft that faintly echoed the sack stench. The night was bitumen black, and my hands ventured out to explore what it was that I was lying on. It felt like fabric stretched over something soft, like human flesh. My fingers found something solid and I kneaded it before screaming out in terror. It was the face of a human being, but it didn't react to my touch. It wasn't breathing. I realized that I was lying on a heap of corpses. Vomit curdled at the back of my throat. I tried to get away, but I couldn't see and was stumbling and falling all over them.

A cackle cracked like a spoon on the lid of my terror and I froze. I knew that cackle well. It was Pungwe.

'So, you're awake,' a rusty voice grated against my ear. I turned in the direction of his voice, only to receive a blunt blow from a hoof hand. 'And you really thought you could escape? After I worked so hard for all of those years to keep you safe, just for me? I am the one who taught you to escape crocodiles. I am the reason that you are who you are, a magic child. And this is how you repay me? By agreeing never to speak to me again?'

A sharp punch struck me in the back, momentarily winding me.

'You tricked me,' my voice was hoarse and low with fear as I tried to ignore the pain tearing into my toe.

Another blow jolted my head, making me bite into my tongue. A salty blood taste bloomed across my mouth.

'I'm a Tokoloshe. It's what I do best,' Pungwe cackled. 'Get up. I'm taking you to my master. We might be able to make a Tokoloshe of you yet. It may be a few days too soon but I am willing to risk it.'

So this was Pungwe's plan. He wanted to make me a Tokoloshe like him. I remembered what Tendai had told me, about the N'anga making him work hard and how he complained of being lonely and wishing he had someone to help him. The hot wetness on my cheeks told me I was crying. I struggled to get to my feet but my knees collapsed beneath me.

'Don't play dumb, Tsoko. Get up,' Pungwe's calloused hooves grappled me to my feet. I stumbled across the pile of dead bodies, feeling bones and flesh giving away beneath me as I trod. The rough hooves prodded me forward. I looked up and above a rim of tears saw the stars spilled endlessly across the sky.

The N'anga

'Master, I have brought her. See?'

The hooves shoved me into a hut that was not dissimilar to Llali's medicine hut. There was a low fire smouldering darkly in the centre, its emaciated shadows dancing across the human skulls that grinned from the walls. Dried snakes hung from the thatch and twirled gently in the warm air currents from the fire. The floor was covered with animal skins that were still half caked in blood.

In the centre of the hut beside the fire, naked except for a coarse, lion-skin skirt, was the N'anga. His hair was matted in long, fat dread locks that drooped dusty down his back. His great meaty body greedily gobbled up most of the space in the hut. Around his neck hung necklaces like Llali's although these ones were made of bones and teeth, and I noticed one that was very similar to the sinister one that Pungwe had given me. My eyes slowly made their way up to his face and when they did, I gasped. There was a long, finger-like bone through the middle of his nostrils, and his lips were pinched around the outsides with the heads of fire ants. His cheeks were tattooed with black arrows that pointed up to his eyes which glowed red as if behind them was a freshly lit fire. I was actually grateful for Pungwe's hooves holding me up or I would have collapsed in terror.

'This? You stupid Tokoloshe, you've been waiting all these years for this?' The N'anga's voice was dangerously low and he spoke as slowly as a python sheds its skin. I felt a shudder of fear ripple through Pungwe.

'She knows magic, master. Good magic. Llali taught her well. I also taught her, master. Everything she has forgotten, I will teach her again,' Pungwe stuttered, stumbling over his words like a pebble tumbling down a mountain.

'And now you want me to take on that pathetic quack's off-cuts as my slave?'

Anger bubbled inside me to hear him call Llali a quack. As if he could detect my thoughts, the N'anga turned his blood-red eyes on me, his eyebrows arched incredulously. I stared back as bravely as I could.

'Scrawny little thing, aren't you?' his lip curled up in a sneer. 'But I suppose you will do. Pungwe is desperate for a playmate and he has had his heart set on you since the day you were born, you know. You owe him. In fact, I'd say you owe him an infinity of grave digging and corpse hauling in that disgusting sack that he carries around. Right, Pungwe?'

A grunting, nervous giggle babbled from behind me before the N'anga picked up a thin, painted reed, aimed it just to the right of my elbow and blew sharply. A dart shot out, brushed past my skin and there was a thud as Pungwe hit the floor behind me with a gravelly squeal.

'Ha. What would I do without these frog-poison darts to paralyse my Tokoloshe? He'll be out for the night now. I can't bear it when he's excited. He will just get in the way. Now let's get on with it.'

My heart jumped into my chest. With Pungwe paralysed, as treacherous as he was, there was no one else but the N'anga and me.

'Come here,' he instructed, darkness brooding behind his face like poisoned ink.

I shuffled tentatively towards him, not wanting to be the second dart victim.

'Turn around,' he ordered. I did as I was told, my legs wobbling pathetically beneath me.

'I don't know what good Pungwe thinks you will be to him. Perhaps he just wants a wife, but I know that lazy little cockroach. He will put you to the toughest work. But you will do. I don't have to waste any of my time training you in magic. And yes, it looks as if I can turn you now. I see you are just starting to blossom. It will be your thirteenth birthday in a few days. Perfect. That makes things very easy for me. Call it an early birthday gift.'

The N'anga unfurled his great body from the bloody rug by the fire and went to collect something from beneath a cluster of rhino horns and elephant tusks propped up against the wall of the hut. As he turned back towards me, I couldn't help the sob that escaped me in a huge, gulping gasp. He was holding a bone that was sharpened at one end to a fine point. The bone was long and slender, like that from a human leg. I knew that it was the bone that the N'anga would use to drive through my forehead. I was about to die and there was nothing I could do. No one would know what had happened. I would be turned into a Tokoloshe and I would be cursed to an eternity of grave digging.

The N'anga considered me with amusement, his red eyes flickering in the low flames. As he walked back towards me, he smacked the sharpened bone against his palm, testing the tip and licking his lips with approval.

'Outside,' he grunted, grabbing my arm tightly in his huge fist and dragging me after him. 'I don't want your mess on my floor.' As he walked past the watery space of air that was Pungwe, the N'anga shot out a sharp kick and there was a responding yelp of pain. I winced.

Outside, the dark air rushed around me. My eyes adjusted quickly, and I saw the pile of corpses that I had woken up on so disoriented a few moments ago. I hadn't noticed the stench of dead flesh then, but now it swelled the air around me. I swallowed back the bile that rose in my throat.

The compound was surrounded by tall, msasa trees, in the centre of which was a crude stone table. On the table was a huge mound of something that I couldn't quite see as it was so dark. Acting as docile as a cat, I worked out the closest tree that would shield me in its shadow. If I could only wriggle free of the N'anga's grip, then I could run to it. I waited for the slightest release on my arm.

It was an elephant's head on the table. While I wanted to cry at the sight of the poor beheaded, detusked beast, I was grateful for it because the N'anga had to let go of my arm as he heaved the great, fleshy head to the floor. Quick as a matchstick striking, I lunged away from him and sped across the compound so fast that my legs hardly touched the ground. The tree was seconds away from me, its great, protective branches beckoning me to safety. I was about to dive into its darkness when I felt a sharp needle of pain lodge itself in my leg and I collapsed into the dust. My leg had lost all sensation and an icy cold sensation seeped through it. In a way, it was a relief as it blotted out the pain in my toe.

'Ha! Do you really think you can escape from the most powerful man in Zimbabwe?' the N'anga gloated as he stood over me, his dart reed in one hand. 'You are lucky you are not yet a Tokoloshe. I can't use the frog poison on a child. It would kill you. But that dart will paralyse you for a few minutes, just the right length of time for me to change you.' He grabbed my arm and dragged me through the dust like a lion with its kill towards the altar again. My heart thudded hopelessly in my chest. Tears squeezed out of my eyes. The N'anga pulled me up into the air by my arm so I hung, flaccid and terrified, from his fierce grip. We were face to face. His bloodied eyes seared deep into me. He then dropped me on the altar, which was still sticky with elephant blood. The iciness of the stone pressed up against my skin. With one hand pressing hard against my chest, he lifted the other holding the bone shard high above his head. I clenched my eyes closed, gritted my teeth and waited to die.

The Boomslang

And then the strangest thing happened. A solitary hiss embroidered the dark air. I had heard that sound before. It was the same sound that I had heard in the lucky bean tree on the day I met Tendai; the warning hiss of the boomslang before it bites its prey.

'YOU!' the N'anga growled, dropping his arm with the sharpened bone to his side. I looked around to see who he was talking to. There was no one.

The N'anga stepped back from me, still gripping the bone-white stake. His eyes turned from blood red to a milky cream colour like boiled eggs in his head.

'Do not interfere, or I will wreak havoc with the ancestors,' the N'anga growled again.

I was confused. Who was he talking to? I followed the direction of his bulging, chalky eyes. They were focused on my legs, and there I saw it, shining like a trickle of green water in the night. Wrapped around my paralysed ankle was the boomslang. My heart fainted in my chest. I didn't stop to wonder where the snake had fallen from, as there were no trees overhanging the stone altar. The boomslang's eyes were not on me, though. They were trained flintily on the N'anga.

'I know who you are,' the N'anga murmured, his voice low and dangerous. 'Don't think you can get away with this.'

The snake continued to watch him beadily. He took another step back, and another and another.

'Go then. You can have her this time. But let me tell you this, you can't protect her forever. Pungwe will find her again.' The N'anga spat and stamped his foot before turning on his heel and walked back into his hut, his dreadlocks swaying like the dried snakes against his naked back.

I turned my eyes back to the boomslang. It was now watching me, and carefully slithering across my leg. I could now feel its hard, cold body against my skin. Sensation was returning. I wriggled my toes. The paralysis was wearing off. The boomslang

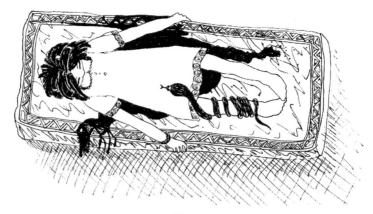

coiled off the stone altar and slithered into the dust to wait a few feet away.

Joy flew into my heart. I suddenly realized that the snake was sent by Llali to rescue me. Why hadn't I realized earlier? The N'anga recognized it as her doing. Just as she had sent a snake to cast a spell on my toe to warn me against Pungwe, she had now sent one to save me from the N'anga. I swung my legs over the side of the stone altar and feebly eased myself onto my feet. My knees and ankles were like jelly, but strength was warming them quickly. I took a step towards the boomslang, and it slithered a little further away. I supposed I was to follow her back to the compound. It waited patiently while I gained my strength, encouraging me slowly forward, step by step, until we had reached the trees. And then it glided, glittery green, through the shrubbery. Eventually I was running, full of terror and joy. I was still alive, I had escaped the N'anga, and didn't the N'anga say that Pungwe was paralysed for the night so wouldn't be able to come after me? I ran as fast as I could after the boomslang towards Llali.

When I reached Llali's compound, it was nearly morning. Stars still peppered the sky, but the birds were starting to hail in the dawn. The boomslang had disappeared into the shrubbery, and I burst into Llali's hut. Llali was there, but she was fast asleep. I scratched my head in confusion. Surely, she would be awake and waiting for me to return? I was too exhausted to worry, though and collapsing on my rug, I dived head first into the deepest sleep ever.

Chipo's Voice

I felt groggy when I awoke, but Llali was there waiting with a hot drink that smelt of acrid herbs. I sipped it gingerly and it unfurled warmly in my chest. I smiled at Llali. My legs ached from running all night, and I felt exhausted from the fear, but I was so happy to be alive.

'Chipo, first see if you can speak.'

'I think I can...'

My voice rang out loudly and strangely around my head, distracting me from the horrors of the previous night.

'I can speak! Llali, I can speak!' I shouted with a grin.

Llali laughed a wheezy laugh. 'You will be talking and talking like a chatter bird for a few days, Chipo. It is good that you have a voice again. But Chipo, what happened to you? It is as if you have been beaten in your sleep. Your body is covered in bruises and there is dried blood on your neck?'

She dabbed at the cuts on my neck and head with some deep red powder from one of the pouches. I winced as it stung my head wounds.

Just as I was about to talk to Llali about what had happened with the N'anga, Babamukuru peeped his head into the hut.

'Ah, she's awake finally. You had a good sleep, Chipo. It's nearly lunchtime, and we need to get back. Everyone will be worried about us, especially Tendai.'

I turned excitedly towards him.

'Babamukuru, I can talk! I can talk!'

A smile broke across Babamukuru's face.

'Ah, Chipo, that is good. Now you can tell me what your real name is. And you can also tell us who your family is so we can take you home, isn't it?'

I panicked. What should I tell him? Surely, I couldn't tell him the truth? I looked to Llali for help. Sadness flickered in her eyes before she spoke up to rescue me.

'It is sad for this little one. Her family was killed. This little girl is the only survivor. She was so shocked by what happened that her memories vanished and she has not spoken since. Trauma is a terrible thing. I have found her voice again, but I cannot find her memories. I think perhaps they are best left hidden. Let her start a new life.'

Babamukuru came over to me and held my hand.

'That is all right, Chipo. You are safe with us.'

With a start, he remembered why he had come to find us.

'Ah, Sangoma! Tandi has also finally woken up. She says she hardly feels any pain! She can't walk yet, but she is smiling again. What did you do for her, Sangoma? How can I repay you for your help?'

'You don't need to pay me, Babamukuru. I am not interested in money. I only ask you to make sure that this little one, I believe you are calling her Chipo, make sure that this little Chipo is well looked after by your people. She is alone in the world and has had a terrible experience. She needs love and security. If you look after her well, it is payment enough.'

'Yes, yes, of course. Amai and Baba are happy to have her. They were going to take care of her until her mother came to collect her. But now I will tell them that she is an orphan. She will be part of my family, too. She saved my daughter's life so I am indebted to her. Our village will be happy to accept her with open arms.'

'You are right, Babamukuru. She saved your Tandi's life. If Chipo had not intervened, your Tandi would surely be dead.' Llali nodded.

Babamukuru knelt down and folded me up into a hug.

'Welcome Chipo. Welcome to our family. You will live with Amai and Baba, but you are always welcome with us,' he said, his voice thick with gratitude.

'Tatenda, Babamukuru,' I said quietly. 'Thank you.'

Babamukuru held me away from him to look at me. 'Listen to you! Such a pretty voice too. Sangoma, you have helped us so much today. To think that you do not expect payment. And the payment you do expect, we would have given gladly anyway.'

Sangoma smiled, but her eyes were heavy with sadness.

'Come, Chipo, it is time to leave. Look, the sun is nearly in the middle of the sky.' Babamukuru beckoned me towards the door.

I looked at Llali, tracing her wise, old face into my memory. My heart sank into my belly as I reached out to take her hand. She gently pulled me towards her and hugged me. 'I am always here for you, always. You will always be my little Tsoko,' she whispered in my ear.

As I waved goodbye out of the rear window of the Peugeot, I saw the silvery thread of a tear slip down her cheek.

Llali was right; I couldn't stop talking. Tandi wanted me to tell her the crocodile story again and again and again. It was a relief not to think about the N'anga or Pungwe. Every time, the crocodile got bigger, the fight more exciting, Tandi braver and myself more heroic. Babamukuru, Tete Precious and Tandi listened generously as I chatted on. Eventually I had spoken myself hoarse. My eyelids grew heavy and I fell asleep.

Returning Home

Tete Precious woke me as we drove into the village. Tendai was sweeping around the fire and when she saw the Peugeot driving in, she ran excitedly towards us.

'Tandi!' she cried, hugging her sister as Babamukuru lifted her out of the back seat.

'Thanks to the Sangoma, she is all right. But it is Chipo who we have to be really grateful to for saving our daughter,' Tete Precious smiled.

Tendai turned tentatively towards me.

'Can you talk?'

'Mmmmm...' I said to test my voice again after my sleep in the car. And then, 'Yes! I have my voice! I can talk!'

My throat and mouth felt so light. It felt wonderful to feel my tongue forming words, my voice lifting from my mouth like butterflies. I laughed happily.

Tendai was desperate to know what had happened and I was desperate to tell her. Everything was happening so fast that I hadn't had any time to think about Pungwe and the N'anga and how Llali had saved me. I relished the thought of mulling over it for hours with Tendai.

After a lunch of sadza, it was agreed that Tendai would walk me back to Amai and Baba's compound. I could not remember the way and needed someone to show me, and we were eager to get away so we could talk freely.

'Do you want me to come with you to tell Amai and Baba what happened, Chipo?' Tete Precious called after us as we hurried towards the path.

'No thank you, Tete Precious. I have my own voice now. I will tell them myself,' I shouted back happily.

Tete Precious agreed. She wanted to tend to Tandi who, while she had improved since yesterday, still needed to be fussed over.

The sun was unfolding a dusty heat across Zimbabwe. Tendai

and I walked in silence for a while until we knew we were out of earshot. Then Tendai turned to me, her eyes wide with anticipation; 'So?' she said, 'Tell me EVERYTHING!'

I blinked at her, wondering where to begin.

'Oh Tendai, the most terrifying thing happened...'

Her face fell.

'What kind of thing?' she asked.

'It's Pungwe. He is the most evil creature. He tricked me.'

'That's not true, Tsoko! Pungwe looked after you. He was like a brother to you! Why would you think that?'

'Tendai, I am just as horrified as you. Llali told me first. She said I should be a normal girl now, without magic, and she did it to save me from Pungwe. Oh Tendai, he was planning on turning me into a Tokoloshe.'

Tendai gasped, her hand clasped over her mouth.

'No! Chipo, do you really believe that?'

I sighed miserably.

'This is going to take a while to tell you...'

Snake Eyes

We were so deep in conversation that we didn't notice a shadow looming ahead of us. Both of us gasped as we almost bumped into the slender figure standing in the middle of the path. We stumbled backwards, grasping onto each other.

'Mangwanani,' the figure said in a low voice.

'Ma...'

I realized who it was before I could finish my greeting. It was Snake Eyes. Up close, I could see that her pupils were so dilated that they made her eyes look like black holes in her head. Goose pimples prickled up against my skin.

'Sipo, you frightened us! What do you want?' demanded Tendai.

Snake eyes didn't take her eyes off me. 'I need to talk to you,' she murmured. Her voice was cool and oily.

'Anything you have to tell Chipo, you can tell me, too,' Tendai snapped, standing in front of me as if to create a barrier between Snake Eyes and me.

'Yes. I want you to hear what I have to say too, Tendai.'

Tendai narrowed her eyes. Snake Eyes reached out her hand to hold my arm. It was icy cold, despite the heat of air around us.

'Who are you?' I asked, pressing myself away from her. 'How do you know me?'

'That is not important now. What is important is that there is a story that needs to be told. And you need to believe it. Come, sit down here, next to me.'

She sat on an old log next to the path and I lowered myself down next to her, keeping a safe distance between us. Tendai perched carefully next to me. We looked at Snake Eyes expectantly.

'This story, it is in the clouds. You must read it right now.'

How did Snake Eyes know I could read clouds?

'Look!' she pointed up at the sky with an urgent finger, her black eyes bulging. I looked at Tendai hesitantly. Tendai nodded and I turned my face up towards the scorched, blue sky and waited for the familiar sky feeling to unfurl through my body.

At first, I didn't see anything. Then Pungwe began to emerge.

'Tsoko!' the words rushed into my ears. Pungwe's voice was pleading, desperate. 'Forget about what happened last night. It was a mistake. And don't listen to Llali! Look at what she did to you! She abandoned you! But I, I have always taken care of you. I am the one you can trust! I will teach you magic again,

Tsoko. I will give you your memories back.' Pungwe's voice rang through my ears.

'Don't listen to Pungwe! Ignore him and look for the story,' Snake Eyes interrupted him angrily.

'No, Tsoko! You cannot ignore me. Don't listen to this Sipo girl. She doesn't know anything. Please, listen to me!'

Snake Eyes grabbed my arm again in her cold grip. 'He is a Tokoloshe. You know he is evil ... look at what happened last night!'

I started. How did Snake Eyes know what had happened? Surely, she had not overheard my conversation with Tendai? Nevertheless, I didn't need to be told to ignore Pungwe.

'NO!' I shouted firmly up at the clouds. 'Leave me alone.'

The horrifying loud wailing screamed through my ears, but this time I knew how to block it. I had to, not only to cut Pungwe off, but also because at this moment I needed to see what the clouds were telling me beyond Pungwe's cries.

I searched the sky carefully, repeating, 'Show me the story that wants to be told.'

Billowing clouds gathered together and a shape began to emerge. It was a woman. She was plump with big smiling face. She was walking through a market. She had two babies cocooned together in a cloth sling on her back. She was singing softly as she walked, her slow steps rocking them to sleep.

'Go to sleep. Go to sleep. My tiny twins, my beautiful, little girls,' she was singing.

I wondered what this had to do with anything. I looked questioningly at Snake Eyes. She was watching me carefully.

'Don't look at me!' she shouted, her black eyes shining. 'Look at the clouds!'

I quickly returned my gaze to the sky.

The woman continued singing to her children, stopping here and there at market stalls to buy tomatoes and spinach, which she put in the basket that was balanced on her head. She left the market and continued to a compound. I guessed this was her home. I followed her inside the kitchen hut where she carefully unloaded the basket of food. She released the cloth that was holding her babies and took the twins gently into her arms.

'There, there, my beautiful twins,' she kept singing to them. The twins slept. The mother lay them to sleep on the reed mat in the kitchen while she tended to the fire and prepared the evening meal, keeping an eye on them as she worked.

Once again, I wondered what this had to do with me. Why was I watching this? But Snake Eyes stare was so intense that it made me feel nervous, so I continued to stare into the clouds.

Then a curious thing happened. I saw something slip into the hut. I couldn't see what it was because it was hiding behind the wooden box where the pots were kept. It then darted behind the cupboard where the tin plates and cups were stored. I didn't like it, this strange creature in the kitchen with the twins. I looked for the mother, but she was outside tending to the fire. She listened closely for any signs of waking, but they were fast asleep. The thing darted out of the shadows, snatched one of the twins, slithered up the wall like a gecko, and was out of the window in a second.

The twin that was left behind started crying, woken by the empty space beside her. The mother bustled into the hut carrying a pot filled with vegetables.

'Don't cry, little mwanas, don't cry,' she was saying. Her eyes took in the missing space where one of her children had been. Her mouth formed a perfect o and she dropped the pot. It clattered at her feet, spilling the tomatoes across the floor.

'What is this? Where is she? Where is Sekai?' the mother cried. She ran around the small kitchen hut, picking up the wooden box to look behind it, looking under the small cupboard. Nothing. She ran around and around, looking in the same places again and again. She was panting with anxiety.

She picked up her other baby, whose wailing was becoming louder, and ran outside. Her eyes were wide with desperation. She ran around the compound shouting for her missing baby. Panic-stricken, she tore at her headscarf and her clothes. 'Tendai, where is your sister? Where is Sekai?' she was shouting again and again.

The babies were too tiny to crawl by themselves, and the mother had been keeping an eye on the door of the kitchen, so she knew no one had entered the hut. Something must have slipped unseen through the tiny window and taken her child. There was no other explanation. She sank to her knees and wailed, her smiling, round face crunched up with tears.

I wanted to cry. I felt the mother's sadness so clearly, but I was confused. Why was I seeing this? Who was this woman and what had taken her baby? What did any of this have to do with me? Was I seeing the future, the past, a dream? I couldn't work it out.

I turned to Snake Eyes.

'Why am I watching this?' I asked.

Snake Eyes' black stare bore into me.

'Have you not figured it out?' she asked slowly.

'Figured what out? What are you talking about?' I asked.

'Chipo, you were that child that was stolen.'

'That was me? I am a twin? So where is my mother? Where is my sister?'

It felt like my life was being shaken around like a rattle and I wished it could stay still for a moment.

Snake Eyes paused. A painful emotion flashed across her face.

'Your mother is dead. Your sister is still alive.'

'How did my mother die?'

'She drowned. She was distraught when she found her daughter, you, missing. She figured out that a Tokoloshe had taken her little Sekai. There was no other explanation. A Tokoloshe was the only thing that could have stolen into the hut unseen. She could not live with the grief that came with imagining what the Tokoloshe had done to her daughter. After searching high and low, she gave up, walked into the river and drowned.'

'Tokoloshe? A Tokoloshe stole me?'

Snake Eyes looked exasperated. 'Chipo, do you still not understand?'

It hit me like a rock. Pungwe had stolen me. Pungwe was the thing that I had seen sneaking through my mother's house. Pungwe had taken me from my sister and my mother. I dropped my head into my hands, just as I started to hear Pungwe's wailing voice again.

'Tsoko, I had to do it. You don't understand. Let me talk to you. I can explain everything.'

I looked up at the sky again. There he was, on his knees holding his hands out to me in desperation. His voice was kneading, pleading. I closed my eyes against him. I turned to

Snake Eyes.

'Why? Why did Pungwe steal me?'

'He stole you because you are a twin. Tokoloshes do not understand the concept of twins; two siblings born at the same time. To a Tokoloshe, twins are like one person. He thought that he could get away with stealing a twin and that your mother would not notice that one of her babies had gone. That way, your mother would not come looking for her missing child. It could have been your sister, but it just so happened that you were closest to the window.'

'So that explains why he took me and not any other baby. But why did he take me in the first place?'

'Pungwe is the N'anga's slave. His work is to dig dead bodies from their graves for the N'anga. The N'anga machetes up the dead bodies to use for muti. Pungwe would try hard to finish his work in the graves, but he could only work at night. The N'anga would get angry because Pungwe couldn't work quickly enough.

So Pungwe had an idea. He would ask the N'anga to create another Tokoloshe to help him and to be his companion and wife. The N'anga hadn't created another Tokoloshe after Pungwe because he couldn't be bothered to train it in magic. Pungwe worked out that if he brought the N'anga a person that already knew magic, the N'anga wouldn't be able to resist. If the person already knew magic, all the N'anga had to do was drive a stake through its head and Pungwe would take care of the rest.

'Pungwe knew that the Sangoma, Llali was barren and childless. She lived alone and wanted someone to share her knowledge with. Pungwe decided that he would steal you and would deliver you to her compound. She is a good Sangoma and he knew that she would take you in as her own and would teach you her magic.

'It worked. The Sangoma found you as if you were an answer to her prayers, a gift from the gods. She started teaching you magic. She taught you how to fly with the birds, so you could go anywhere you wished. She gave you absolute freedom and, by doing so, played straight into Pungwe's trap.

'Pungwe chose his moment well. You were lonely. It was before you knew Tendai. You had no friends except for Llali. One day, as you were playing by the river, Pungwe appeared to you as a little boy. He knew that you would run away if he appeared as himself, as an ugly Tokoloshe. He befriended you and you began to trust him and love him like a brother.'

I felt weak. Sipo's story matched everything that I had witnessed at the N'anga's compound. All along, he had been plotting to make me into a Tokoloshe like him. No wonder he had rescued me from the crocodile! He didn't want me to die before the time was right to present me to the N'anga.

Tendai squeezed my hand.

'When Llali found out, she was devastated. She loved you like her own child, and she knew immediately what Pungwe was up to as soon as she found out that he worked for the bad N'anga. She had no choice but to take away your memory of magic, not only so you couldn't see Tokoloshes anymore, but also so Pungwe would lose interest in you. And she took your voice, just in case he managed to find a way to talk to you. That way you wouldn't be able to speak to him.

'She found Amai and Baba who desperately wanted a child and she delivered you to them in the afternoon while Amai was sleeping. It was the only thing she could do.'

Tendai put her arm around my shoulders as I broke into sobs. There was so much to take in.

'You said my sister is still alive? Where is she?'

'Yes, your sister is still alive. Did you not hear the names your mother used? You were Sekai, your sister was Tendai. That is who your sister is. Tendai.'

'Tendai? This Tendai? My sister? My twin? But her mother is Tete Precious!'

'Yes, her mother is Tete Precious now. Tete Precious is your aunt. She took care of your sister once your mother drowned herself. There was no one else. Tete Precious has a kind heart. She could not turn away her sister's baby.'

I turned to look at Tendai. She nodded, her eyes wide with disbelief.

'What she says is true. I was an orphan and Tete Precious took me in. I don't remember a time before her so she became my mother.'

I shook my head. Could we really be twins? I supposed that even though Tendai was taller than me, there were similarities in our faces. Our eyes were the same shape and our cheeks had the same curve. And we always had the same thoughts. I held up my hand and indicated for her to do the same. We pressed our palms together. They were exactly the same size.

We blinked at each other in amazement.

I turned to Snake Eyes again.

'There is something missing. How do you know all of this? Who are you?'

'I knew you would ask that. It is difficult to explain. Remember the snake in Amai's dream? And the one on the path the night you went to the neighbour's compound? And remember the boomslang by the lucky bean tree? It would never have bitten either one of you. That snake was me. I am the one who introduced you to your sister, because I knew that you needed each other. And did you not wonder about the boomslang last night that lead you back to safety?'

Tendai and I exchanged looks again. Suddenly my eyes widened in recognition. I remembered the boomslang's giant, black eyes. Snake Eyes had exactly the same. But she was not sent by Llali, surely? So who was she?

Tendai turned to me and said slowly, 'Tsoko, you once told me that snakes were our link to the ancestors, to the spirit world. Their bellies slide along the ground, the world of the living while their backs are bared to the sky, to the realm of the ancestral spirits. Sipo is telling us that she is a link to the spirit world.'

'Yes, Tendai, that is right. You have grown up to be a bright little one, haven't you?'

I then remembered what the old sekuru said about the snake on the path, on my first night here. He said that the snake had a message from the ancestral spirits.

My head swung around in disbelief.

'You are our mother?'

Snake Eyes sighed.

'I am your mother's spirit, yes, but I have taken over Sipo's body just as I took over the snakes' bodies. I had to; at least until I knew that my girls are safe. Some people are better spirit carriers than others, and Sipo is one of those people. Most importantly, the reason I had to do this is because it will be your thirteenth birthday soon. That is when Pungwe was planning to kill you. But I see that he got to you before then.'

Tete Precious had mentioned that Tendai's birthday was coming up, and if we were twins, that made us the same age. I shivered. Tokoloshes could not be created from the corpses of children. They had to be at least thirteen years old.

'My girls, I can't stay any longer. This body belongs to Sipo and she must continue with her life. I have done what I came to do. It is time for me to go.'

She grasped our arms tightly. Her eyes were dark and dilated, looking at Tendai and me in turn.

'My twins,' her voice was a whisper. 'My beautiful twins.'

She pulled away from us and crouched on the ground with her eyes closed. Tendai and I looked at each other. Neither of us knew what to do. Moments passed, and I put my hand on Sipo's shoulder. She jolted as if she had woken suddenly from a long sleep. She turned to look at us, disoriented and confused.

'What am I doing here? What has happened?' Her eyes were no longer dilated. Poor Sipo, she had no idea of the strange stories she was telling us moments ago. I quickly thought of an explanation.

'Nothing has happened. We found you here, sleeping near this log. We were on our way home. We wanted to sit with you to make sure you were safe while you slept. There are many snakes in this area.'

Sipo shook her head. She looked confused and bewildered.

'Tatenda. Thank you, my friends. I will return the favour one day.'

We bid her farewell and started back towards Amai's compound. Tendai looked at me.

'Did that just happen? Tsoko, did that really just happen?'

'Yes. I think it did. It makes sense, though, doesn't it? You are my sister, my twin. I know that is true.'

'Me too. But Pungwe? I can't believe he is evil after all.'

'I know.'

I shook my head, and then I turned to grin at my sister. 'But I am still here. You are still there. The sky is still blue. That is all that matters. Isn't it?

'Yes. That is all that matters.'

Shona Glossary

Ambuya — grandmother
Chengerai — danger
Compound — gathering of huts
Duiker — small deer
Iwe — you
Garwe — crocodile
Mwana — baby
Moroi — Hello
Maiwe! — exclamation of surprise
Mealie — corn
Mealie meal — corn ground into powder
Muti — magic medicine
N'anga — male witch doctor
Relish — stew
Sadza — ground corn cooked with water, similar to polenta
Sangoma — female witch doctor
Sekuru — grandfather
Shamwari — friend
Shiri Yakanaka Uno Ende Pi — Pretty bird, where are you going?
Tatenda — thank you
Tete — aunt
Toitoi — danced

**OUR STREET
BOOKS**

Our Street Books for children of all ages, deliver a potent mix of
fantastic, rip-roaring adventure and fantasy stories to excite the
imagination; spiritual fiction to help the mind and the heart
grow; humorous stories to make the funny bone grow; historical
tales to evolve interest; and all manner of subjects that stretch
imagination, grab attention, inform, inspire and keep the pages
turning. Our subjects include Non-fiction and Fiction, Fantasy
and Science Fiction, Religious, Spiritual, Historical, Adventure,
Social Issues, Humour, Folk Tales and more.